Foreclosed

A Mitzy Neuhaus Mystery

Foreclosed

Traci Tyne Hilton

Foreclosed: A Mitzy Neuhaus Mystery
Proverbs 31 House LLC
Copyright 2009 (5/13 LD)
All rights reserved
Cover Photograph by Michael Rothery
Cover Design by Andrew Rothery

Foreclosed

Dedicated to Daniel, Norah, and Lucy, who love stories.

Foreclosed

Chapter One

Mitzy Neuhaus pulled her desk chair up to the microphone. The radio booth was small, and Johnny, her host, nudged her with his elbow, and smiled. Mitzy slipped her headphones on.

Johnny Headly, host of the morning show on the local Christian talk radio station began his morning chatter. "Hey, Mitzy, baby. How's the real estate business?" It was the same every Wednesday morning.

She smiled her wide, bright smile. "Business is good, John. Not fast, not hectic, not for the fearful, but good."

"How can it be good, Mitz?"

"It's not perfect, of course." Mitzy shifted in her seat. "But there are great deals and brilliant Realtors ready to find you one. If you have some equity or savings and are ready to make a move, the best Realtors are reading and waiting." Mitzy wasn't just putting a good spin on a bad economy. If only people would grab the houses while they could, Realtors could save the economy.

"Mitzy is ready and waiting? That sounds too good to be true," Johnny drawled.

Mitzy cringed. How did he manage to make that sound so dirty? "Ready and waiting—to sell a house, Johnny." She wished the radio audience could see her roll her eyes. "It's all about the money, friend. If you need to get out of your house, a good Realtor can still make you some money. And good Realtors are available."

"Mitzy, I've been dying to know for years; are you available? And can I change that?"

"If you need your house sold, John, I'm your girl. Anything else…well, leave your card with my assistant." Mitzy scrunched her nose at Johnny.

He winked.

"But speaking of experienced professionals in the homes industry, I want to spotlight my professional peers who work tirelessly in the mortgage business."

"Not those devils that wrecked the economy."

"Of course not! The economic crisis has sifted the wheat, and the chaff has blown away. The sub-prime creative loan element has been kicked to the curb." Mitzy leaned in to the mic and lowered her voice. "But rates are sooo low. If you have any equity, my friends can save you some serious cash each month. I have links on my website to my recommended lenders." Mitzy leaned back in her desk chair and popped her shoulders. She could run on about the industry forever.

John gave her the keep going signal.

"Listen, it's 2008. Interest rates are less than five percent. Don't sit there with a 2007 mortgage at seven percent. That's foolish."

"Preach it, sister." Johnny nodded his head in time to music only he could hear.

"My job for you all today is this: consider the terms of your current loan, contact your local credit union or check out the links on my website, and see if they can do better for you. It is always the right time to save tens of thousands of dollars."

"Thank you, Mitzy. You make common sense look real good." Johnny chuckled.

"Thank you?" Mitzy laughed. "I know I talk sense, but if it were common, I don't think our economy would be in such a mess."

With that her spot was over. She turned off her microphone, waved through the window at the producer, and slipped out of the booth.

Johnny read the police reports from the Vantage Heights neighborhood for a few quick laughs.

Mitzy didn't laugh when she thought of Vantage Heights.

Yes, they called the police when the new neighbor put up a basketball hoop and yes, they called 911 when someone parked a Kia on their block, but too many of them were losing their homes because they never should have bought them in the first place.

Foreclosed

She stifled a laugh as she left the radio station. The week Vantage Heights biddies called 911 on the neighbor who planted corn in the front lawn was pretty funny. But those old biddies weren't the ones losing their homes.

The radio station was hurting now, the same way all the local businesses were hurting. Advertising dollars were short all around. As Mitzy pounded the pavement back to her penthouse, she thought it was probably a good time to negotiate for a better spot.

She wanted a larger audience share, but she didn't have the time to be on the radio everyday. She considered the Saturday morning line-up. They called it 'The Fix-it Show.' She could seriously improve that program. If it was Neuhaus' All Things New Show or maybe Fixing Your House with Neuhaus, they could keep all of their regular programming and add another spot for her.

But owning the fix-it weekend wasn't exactly right either. Mitzy wanted to inform and educate and there just weren't enough people listening to the radio these days.

And then Mitzy knew.

She went straight home and sat down for a late breakfast with her Tivo-ed morning shows. She savored her cup of coffee as she evaluated the *First Things with Alma and Bob*. They were funny. They were local. They seemed to have their fingers on the pulse of town. Mitzy had always liked their show.

Everything on their program clicked, except they skirted around the issue of the failing economy. They needed Mitzy and her keen real estate sense. *First Things with Alma and Bob* was exactly where she needed to be. She tucked this tid-bit into the back of her mind, cleared her dishes and made her way to the office, just on time, for a Wednesday.

Sabrina, Mitzy's assistant, sat at her computer studying the multiple listing service site for any recent activity.

Ben, the graphics artist, was sketching something in his pad. It made no difference to Mitzy what he was working on, but it probably had something to do with his web design consulting.

Joan, the stager Mitzy loved the best, was in just to chat, but found that there was nothing to talk about.

Mitzy paced the room, drumming her pencil on her fist, and chewed on the idea of breaking into television.

Sabrina would be of use in whatever she did. Ben's work probably wouldn't increase, but if she could increase confidence in the marketplace, all of their regular work would return to normal.

Joan.

She appraised her friend closely. Joan was artistic, no doubt. She was also well-spoken. Mitzy could put Joan on the air in her morning show segment, and Joan could get commission work from the exposure.

There was nothing wrong with her television idea, as far as she could tell.

"Sabrina, I need a proposal. We need to get our Neuhaus New Homes Spotlight onto *First Things with Alma and Bob*."

"Ooh, I like that idea," Joan said. "Mitzy, that's just the right medium for you. You could spotlight some of your favorite houses, give tours, everything."

"I could," Mitzy said.

"But you have something else in mind." Joan raised an eyebrow and leaned in close.

"I think that this town needs to relax and gain confidence in their ability to survive the crisis. They really can survive, you know." Mitzy swept her arm out towards the city on the other side of the window, longing to give them all a hand up.

"Marketplace confidence through *First Things*? Really, Mitz? We have twelve percent unemployment right now. Who cares what Alma and Bob think about it?" Ben rocked back in his desk chair.

"Ah, but, Ben, that's close to the same thing as eighty-eight percent employment." Mitzy chewed on the end of her pencil. "There are a lot of people out there with secure jobs, and the ability to invest in their town. They've just got to realize they can do it themselves."

"You can call the show *Bootstrapping with Mitzy the Republican*." Ben smirked.

"It's not a political idea, Benjamin." Mitzy shook her head. "Let's say your business has just received some money, stimulus money." Mitzy sat down on the edge of her desk. "Say you are building a new community center. The people in charge need to view that money, not in the light of how much building they can get for it, but as how far they can spread the money into the economy, to create more jobs." Mitzy's heart was racing, her face was heating up. It was one of her personal goals to make Ben less of a pessimist.

"Yeah, yeah. We all know that already."

"But it's the same for people who have savings and business reserves. This is the time to spend our money employing people." Mitzy started pacing again and drumming her purple fingernails on her tightly clenched fist. "The segment needs to be fun, and touring homes is fun. But it has to increase consumer and investor confidence, or it is completely worthless."

The phone rang. Sabrina jumped at the sound. "Neuhaus New Homes. This is Sabrina speaking, how may I help you?" She wore her big smile as she spoke. It was Neuhaus policy; the person on the other line could hear the smile. "Thank you, can you hold?"

She covered the receiver with her palm and looked up at Mitzy with a little fear in her eyes. "It's Alonzo."

Mitzy grimaced. She had a desk in the front with her staff, but she also had a private office where she could sign papers with clients. She rarely did other business in that office. She turned on her heel and disappeared into it now.

"I've quoted you the lease terms at least three times, Alonzo. You know what it will take to get into my office space." Mitzy sat on the edge of her desk chair. She had to stay calm.

"Let's be realistic, Neuhaus. I want to own the whole building, and you know it. I'll say a number right now that you can't refuse. Then you can take your little office friends back to the suburbs."

Foreclosed

"It's not for sale." Mitzy spit the words out. Who was this man to call her business 'little office friends'? She knew without a doubt that her bottom line was better than his.

"Everything is for sale."

Mitzy took a deep breath. "My tenants need security right now. I am not going to make a move that would threaten their businesses."

"Who's talking about threats? I'm talking money, and a lot of it."

"That's enough. We've had this same conversation three times. I'm not selling. You don't have enough money to tempt me to put my tenants out on the street."

"You're location is perfect for me. Access to building supplies. Access to transportation. Your little street-front shops might have to move, but new tenants would move in and that would be good too. There's no end of space for little music shops and crafty places." Alonzo's voice was suave but it set Mitzy's teeth on edge.

"If you need office space you can have the whole top floor. It's yours. You know my lease terms are fair." Mitzy closed her eyes and prayed for patience. It was his tone that really had her. He talked to her like she was a child.

"Maybe if you'd *sell* me the top."

"It's not for sale. I own this building and that won't change."

"I'm not in a rush, Mitzy. We'll talk about this again."

Mitzy pinched her mouth shut.

"Now, don't be upset. Just think of all the shoes you could buy when you sell out to me."

Mitzy stood up. "Thank you for your interest in my property. I'm pleased to know that I have something of value. If you are interested in a lease, feel free to call again."

Alonzo was silent for a moment. "Oh, we'll talk."

Mitzy didn't want to be the first to hang up. She waited a half a second longer. "Would you like me to let you know if I hear of a similar property for sale?"

Alonzo laughed. "You'd be my buyer's agent?"

"We could work something like that out." Mitzy licked her lips. Was he coming around?

"Oh, darlin', I have friends in real estate with licenses older than you. Now, don't get all bent out of shape. My offer is solid. Lots of money. I'll call back later and I think you'll be glad I did." He hung up.

Bent out of shape! Mitzy stomped around the room, from corner to corner. Bent out of shape! Every month for the last three months he had called her and gotten the same answer. Of course she was bent out of shape. Her building was Not. For. Sale.

Alonzo thought Mitzy and her building had a lot in common, they both weren't as young as they used to be, and were highly overrated.

Unfortunately for Alonzo, he believed that Mitzy's building was the exact size, location, and opportunity that he needed right now.

Alonzo knew Mitzy was a successful Realtor. Twenty prime location billboards and a regular radio feature don't lie. When he realized the housing bubble had burst, he had hoped Mitzy needed to liquidate so he could buy the building he'd had his eye on for so long.

Unfortunately for him, it appeared that she had resources to carry her through the storm.

Buying one story would have worked, he supposed, if she hadn't been so cocky about it. She wouldn't even listen to his offer!

The property was all wrong for her business, and just right for his. If she had been willing to listen, she would have heard an offer she couldn't refuse.

He stared at his phone. His head had begun to pound. He knit his eyebrows together. What was wrong with that woman, and why would she not sell him her stupid office building?

Mitzy had no time for vain or condescending men. It was an insult to be asked to sell her building, even part of it.

Would he have tried that with the Moyer family, who owned a stretch of Downtown Portland? She thought not.

She may only own one commercial property, but it was hers and hers alone and she was keeping it.

She stared out the back window. It might not be the best location for Tabby's ceramic studio, but backing to the stoneworks plant and the lumber mill was priceless to her as a home renovator and probably the only reason Alonzo Miramontes was speaking to her.

She sighed. It would be different if Alonzo had treated her like a professional peer. She knew of one other building on her block that would have suited him, but only she knew how tight the owner's situation was.

If Alonzo Miramontes had been decent to her, he could have benefited from her knowledge.

But not now.

She opened the door to the main office, careful to project a confident, unrattled appearance. There was no need to let her employees know how much that man could unsettle her.

"It's a bit too quiet here this morning. Let's start working on the suite upstairs. Apparently some people will believe this building is for sale until I get a tenant in it," Mitzy said, abandoning her television career for the moment.

Joan picked up her sketch pad, a twinkle in her eye.

Ben opened his AutoCAD program.

Sabrina opened her Word file.

"Is there room in the foyer to add an elevator shaft?" Mitzy asked Ben.

"I don't have a blueprint here, but if you don't mind losing a lot of your entry space on the first floor I think there is room."

"That's what I thought, and I am pretty sure, though I don't specialize in commercial real estate," there was a snide tone in her voice, "that we would have to put one in if we did any major upgrades."

Sabrina took notes in her own computer short hand. She kept typing as she spoke. "I can get the requirements and code today."

"Perfect. I don't want to lease the entire upstairs to one company. It makes more sense to create two large spaces or one large, one medium, and one small. Joan, have you ever thought of having an office outside of your home? It sure would be nice for us to have you close at hand."

Joan narrowed her eyes and smiled. "I have thought of it. But there hasn't been anything available in this area. Right now my van is my office when you get right down to it."

"I can rent this space as quickly as we can have it ready, however, I'd like to let you have one of the suites." Mitzy templed her fingers. "You know what would be cool? If you were the Neuhaus stager. We could make you a more permanent part of the team."

"I do have some thoughts on that." Joan chewed her bottom lip. "One reason I'd like to have an office space would be so I could interview potential clients outside of Neuhaus work, especially right now while things are slow. Why don't I draw up a proposal and we can talk about it?"

Mitzy knew that Joan, being an artist, had no great desire to draw up proposals, but she appreciated the professional approach Joan was taking. "Sounds good. Have it ready by tomorrow, lunch. I'll bring some ideas on how we could arrange it as well."

"I think, excepting the elevator, the renovation could be finished by the end of the month." Mitzy turned to her graphics guy. "Ben, I'd like you to get started on the advertising. Make sure to emphasize the multiuse location, perfect for builders and remodelors, perfect for professionals, etc. You know what I want."

Ben smiled at his computer, he knew. She wanted it perfect and with a lot of purple. And with the name Neuhaus on it about a million times. Her methods worked, even if they weren't the sophisticated Wall Street look he had preferred at Uni. "Can do."

"Sabrina, first, get the proposal for *First Things*, put together. Email it to me by end of day. Make the permits second priority. We have the rest of the week to work on them." Mitzy sat down at her desk, slipped on her reading glasses and opened her email. It would take a good hour to get through her correspondence, but communicating with clients and fans was something she never passed off to her assistant.

The phone rang again. They all jumped this time.

"Pathetic," Ben said.

In their office the phones used to ring more than they were silent. In fact, they had more phone lines than people. Managing the phones was a point of pride for Sabrina. No one could handle eight callers at once like her.

"Good afternoon, Neuhaus New Homes, this is Sabrina speaking. How can I help you? Oh, I see, Just a moment." She put the caller on hold. "Mitzy, it's the renter at your Baltimore Street house."

Mitzy nodded and picked up her extension. "This is Mitzy, how are things, Deb? Umm hmm…yes. Really?" Mitzy's voice rose with excitement. "That's terrific, thanks. No, I think I'll get over there right away. Thanks for calling. Talk to you soon."

Foreclosed

All eyes were on Mitzy. It had been a while since a promising call came in.

"Well?" Sabrina said.

"The Victorian is going into foreclosure!" Mitzy's big blue eyes sparkled with excitement.

"The Baltimore Victorian?" Joan asked.

"Deb said movers were there last night, late. This morning all of the cars were gone and the house was dark."

"No kidding? We've wanted that house for ages." Joan and Mitzy had longed for the old house on Baltimore Street. The perfect bones of a Queen Anne Victorian mansion were like chocolate to Joan—irresistible. The investment potential of that property was almost too much for Mitzy.

Mitzy dreamed of restoring it to its historic glory and selling it to someone with old money. There was always a market for the historically minded, since the best locations were so rarely for sale.

It was a great investment for Mitzy personally as well. The street was zoned commercial/residential. The big Victorian would make as great an office building as it would a home. But an office would not protect the value of Mitzy's other Baltimore Street property. A restored vintage mansion, preferably on the historic register, would protect her property values nicely.

"I knew this market had to be good for somebody," Ben moaned. Rehabbing an old house didn't involve him until the very end.

"Pause the proposal, Sabrina. We need to take a trip to Baltimore Street."

"It's not listed yet." Sabrina scanned the multiple-listing service for the address.

"No, but it's vacant. Let's get to it before the no trespassing signs go up. Who knows what condition it's in after all this time?"

Foreclosed

Chapter Two

"Baltimore Street needs a bed and breakfast. This house would be perfect for it," Sabrina said.

"It would be, but I don't want to be the one who sets that precedent on Baltimore. Imagine instead, what it would be like if one of Aerin and Brett's foundation friends moved in. They'd keep an immaculate garden. They'd keep the house painted. It could be a showpiece to the right family."

Mitzy hadn't quite broken into her sister-in-law's grant giving set yet. One big sale like this would open up a world of future sellers and buyers. The granting-grants set lived in a different part of town and tended to handle real estate through their lawyers, but Mitzy was confident that, if she had the right property, she could gain their confidence. Old money called her name. She would love to sell to old money.

"It would be a coup, Mitzy, but really, would it be that much better than scones and biscuits and gravy and hash browns? And fresh fruit?

And gourmet coffee? And fluffy, soft, satin comforters and gas fireplaces in every room? And newspapers at your door…and cable TV? Cable is always better when you are staying somewhere else." Sabrina gazed into the far distant future as she described her dream getaway.

"And a handsome young Jorge to do turn-down service?" Mitzy beeped her Miata open. It was red. She often thought of having it repainted purple, but that could wait until it showed its age a little more. They kept talking as they slipped in and zipped away.

"That wouldn't hurt." It had been a couple of years since Sabrina had been out, handsome Jorge or not.

"It is a great idea. And if I didn't already own a Baltimore property, I'd consider it. I know the neighborhood pretty well. The neighbors keep it up. They haven't aged out yet. Most aren't even baby boomers. They have kids in school and seem to want to stay put. I'd hate to be the first person that put a business on their street. Find yourself a different dream vacation, please. Let's rescue this mansion and sell it to some lovely snobby couple who will never let it run to ruin."

"Maybe, if they can be lovely, not snobby people."

"I'll see what I can do." Mitzy had her mind on the upcoming Dinner with Degas event at the museum. She had been invited to the annual fundraiser, as usual. And, as usual, was expected to politely decline. In fact, she was usually offered two tickets to whatever event was up and coming and was always expected to give them to her parents. She was trying to remember why this had become the expectation. She supposed it was because she didn't have anyone to bring. She drove less carefully than

Sabrina liked, as she tried to remember the slip of conversation about this year's event…what had it been…?

Oh, yes. Perfect.

They pulled into the driveway of Mitzy's Baltimore rental. The Victorian was set back from the road with a tree lined drive that had a turn around. The home had sat alone on the road once, with acres around it. At some point the land had been parceled out and sold for ranch homes to accommodate young, not so rich, families.

There was some work that needed doing on the outside. The landscaping, forget about it. It was a wreck. She'd call Martin and his crew for a bid. The exterior needed painting, and probably needed shingles replaced. The house could do with new cedar shakes on the roof as well. Not so bad, she was sure, compared to what it needed inside. Considering the worn down exterior, she imagined it had been a few decades since the interior had been redone.

The girls slipped out of the car and waved to Deb, who was watching them from her picture window. Sabrina had an easier time on the mud and gravel driveway in her Birkenstocks than Mitzy, in her heels, did. Mitzy didn't mind running back and forth to work in her heels, but the sticking mud wasn't her idea of fun. She scraped them off on the edge of the concrete steps.

"Stamped concrete or pavers?" she asked Sabrina.

"Pavers. It's more true to the original."

"You're right. I just like my concrete supplier too much to admit it." She put her shoes back on and joined Sabrina in window peeping. She did like her concrete supplier. Too bad he was married. Johnny at the radio station wasn't married. Was he really as obnoxious as he seemed? Was he really interested in her?

"Ooh! Look at the parquet entry! It's so shiny!" It was hard to see beyond the entry. The entry itself, however, was well lit from the foyer windows. The shine on the floor made her think it had been restored and maintained. They snuck around to the side windows next.

"The kitchen must be on this side," Mitzy said.

"Sure is. My lands!" Sabrina was on her tiptoes trying to get a good view into the house.

Mitzy peeked in the same window. "Is that a professional, stainless steel range?"

"I'm sure it is," Sabrina said. "But what on earth is it doing in this house?"

"Apparently being a matched set with the rest of the stainless appliances and—it cannot be." Mitzy stopped short, amazed at what she saw.

"I think it is." Sabrina's voice was reverently quiet.

The sun was shining just right to glance off the countertops with an appealing sparkle.

"That is a quartz countertop," Sabrina said.

"Acres and acres of quartz countertop. Well, we know why they were foreclosed now, I guess. Just plain ran out of money. Let's get back to the office. You get the tax records on the house and I'll call James at the stoneworks and see what he knows."

They risked a ticket as they sped back to the office. They were out of sight before you could read MIT-Z on the Miata's vanity plates.

Alonzo paced back and forth in his office. His stride was long, which frustrated his pacing in the small room. He bumped his secretary's desk every time he passed it.

His secretary cursed him under her breath. Every bump of the desk tipped her coffee cup. Cleaning the mess was a bother, but at this rate she'd have to make another pot before she could really wake up for the day.

"How is the Steinfeld's project?"

"Finished, sir."

"I know that. But how do they feel about it? What kind of message are they sending future clients? What do you think we can make out of it?" His thick black eyebrows were drawn in concentration. His hands moved nervously through his black hair, making it stand on end.

"It was months ago, sir. I think if we were going to get any residual business from the pickle job, we would have heard by now."

"Nonsense. This is a slow economy, all the processes slow down. Put some feelers out, will you?"

Marge made a note on the pad next to her phone and nodded vigorously as though she intended to do just that with her feelers.

Alonzo had given most of his staff a lengthy vacation the week before, so all of his pent up energies were being spent on poor Marge, who wanted nothing more than to drink her coffee and read celeb gossip online.

"Al, why don't you move forward with your plans for the office? You have the time and the men now." Marge cradled her coffee cup under her nose as she spoke. She didn't want to ruin everything on her desk just because her boss was restless.

"Harrumph," was all Alonzo offered in reply.

"Haven't you been talking to those Neuhaus people? I bet you could snap that office suite up in a second. We could be renovated and moved in by mid-summer."

"I wouldn't share space with that *Realtor* if it was the last building in town." He abandoned his secretary and his office, and slammed the door behind him.

Marge sighed with satisfaction. She settled down in her chair with her mug and opened Firefox. "Men," she muttered.

He jumped into his Hummer and hit the road—action being preferable to inaction.

He pulled his Hummer out into traffic and swung into the far lane.

He made a wide left turn.

Horns blared as he weaved into the far lane again.

He was seeing red—seeing nothing else but the unendurable frustration of stupid people and women who wouldn't be reasonable. His head slammed into the windshield— "What the?" The world went black.

Two blocks back, two women in a red Miata sat, tapping their toes anxiously, thinking up alternate routes back to work. Sabrina pulled her Blackberry out of her knapsack and started typing.

"I don't know why I always forget about this thing."

"We're getting old, Brinsie. We don't think of using a telephone to pull up tax records. You do that and I'll call James while we wait. I suppose we could have done this at the property. We might have even gotten inside if we had stayed there." Mitzy shook her head. Slow business made her careless.

No one answered at the stoneworks place. As soon as she had inched forward far enough, Mitzy turned right into an alley. She didn't care to know what the accident ahead was about. It seemed to her that a stop off at Annie's Donuts was in order. Guys that work with stones like to eat donuts, And, she bet, they would be happy to answer questions about recent jobs over a friendly cup of coffee and those same donuts.

"Here it is, Mitzy. It says here that the house is owned by a guy called Laurence Mills. He must have wanted to be a flipper. He bought it earlier this year from someone called Maxim Mikhaylichenko. I wonder why Maxim sold without remodeling it first."

"Sabrina, really. Not all Russians are builders."

"I'm not being rude, Mitzy, I swear. I know not all Russians are builders. But all Russians know Russian builders. It just seems odd that someone with connections would sell a property in bad condition."

"Sabrina! Connections? Listen to yourself," Mitzy said.

Foreclosed

"For Heaven's sake, I didn't mean like the Godfather." Sabrina tapped the screen of her Blackberry, looking for more information.

"Anyway, he might not be Russian, he might not know any builders, or he might not have had any money. There are plenty of reasons why Maxim Whatshisname might not have fixed the house up before he sold it." Mitzy had seen everything in this business and wasn't ready to pigeonhole the previous owner because of his name.

"Or…it could be a Soprano's thing. Maybe the sale was a cover of some sort," Sabrina said with a grin.

Mitzy pulled into a parking spot in front of Annie's Donuts. "Run inside and buy a dozen of the best." Mitzy handed Sabrina her wallet with a grin. "We'll find out what we need to know."

The two beautiful women and their box of donuts received a warm welcome from their hungry male friends inside the stoneworks shop.

"Victorian on Baltimore?" James said with a mouth full of donut. "I don't recall. Did you work on that one, Bruce?" Bruce was negotiating his donut into his coffee and offered a grunt.

"What kind of work did they get done?' James washed his maple bar down with a swallow of coffee.

"We saw quartz counters in the kitchen. There may have been bathroom work done as well. It looked like there was nothing doing for landscaping though." Mitzy leaned forward, elbows on the table, unconsciously giving the impression that she hung on their every word. It was disarming to the men and when combined with the donuts, a powerful tool for their memory.

"We did a quartz job about a month ago, didn't we?"

"Yeah," Bruce offered. He helped himself to a crueller.

"Did we do the install?"

"Yeah."

"Was it in the Eastside?"

"Yeah, over on Baltimore." Their buddy Tony wiped his hands on his blue jeans and grabbed a donut as he passed the table.

Mitzy leaned in a little closer. "Will you be doing more work at that property?"

"No." That was from Bruce.

"The guy didn't pay, of course. And now he's in bankruptcy. A real pain in the, well. A real pain. That was an awesome slab of rock he bought and it's gonna sit in the house and rot until the bank does something about it. Probably next year." James seemed to remember the whole thing now.

"Oh dear," Sabrina murmured with a half frown. She let her gaze drop to her coffee as Bruce looked her way.

"Unless there was a buyer for the house." Mitzy was already planning how to fix this for her friend and his business.

"You all have a lien on the property. If a traditional sale goes through on it you'd be paid first."

"You got some buyers hiding upstairs at Neuhaus?" Bruce asked with a laugh.

Foreclosed

Mitzy was thinking about the Dinner with Degas. It was definitely time to buy an evening gown and find a date for the upcoming event. "Where my buyers are hiding is a secret I won't even tell you friends."

She nodded goodbye and walked out of the stoneworks office, pleased with a job well done. She was sure that this was a failed flip job and an upcoming foreclosure. If she could get along with Aerin for one evening…or possibly two, she could fix it all.

Sabrina gave one last longing look at the donut box and then followed her boss out.

Alonzo sat in the emergency room on his bed getting madder by the moment.

Concussion.

Whiplash.

A bleeding traffic ticket.

The ticket was the last thing he needed. His car was likely totaled. Why drive a Hummer if it can get totaled by a…what had that been? Oh. An armored car from the US treasury. A ticket for reckless driving was probably getting off lightly. He came to pretty quickly, though his head still hurt like well, like hell. He was trying to cut out the swearing but some things were just too much. And if Pastor Hank could say hell, so could Alonzo. Especially after totaling his car two months before it was paid off.

The hospital didn't seem in any hurry to let him out. Sitting in this room was making him livid, and the madder he got the worse his head hurt. He pressed his nurse call button three more times. Where the…had his nurse gone? *Not much better than actually swearing,* he thought. *Sorry, Lord.*

Thinking with God in mind had been an easier habit to develop than on his knees praying, which he never did much of. He didn't do much of anything formally now that he was a Christian. But maybe he'd better.

The hope he had that God would help him get control over his anger had been a big selling point for the born-again thing. He caught a glance of himself in the mirror. Both his forehead and his cheek were purple with bruises. He was lucky his head hadn't gone through the windshield.

The nurse came in, looking as annoyed as he felt. "Yes?" she said without making eye contact.

"Am I getting out of here?" He spoke through gritted teeth, but at least he spoke and didn't yell.

"Not likely. Is that all?"

"No it is not all. Where is the doctor and why am I not getting out of here?"

"The doctor is with emergency patients, sir." Sir sounded like an insult when she said it. "He will see you as soon as he is able. In the meantime, he would like you to lie down and rest, but try not to fall asleep. Would you like the television on?" She picked up the remote and turned on the TV. The noise hit him like a wall; he doubled up and barfed all over the floor.

Foreclosed

He was pretty sure if he sat up his head would fall off, but he heard the nurse pull the curtain around his bed as she left. He closed his eyes and hoped the janitor would come quickly, or the smell of the vomit would make him do it again.

After clean up and much consultation with the doctor on rotation and the regular doctor, he was given the bed for the afternoon, some pain medication and the same caution against falling asleep.

The television was just too much for him so he turned on the radio.

It had been a day of interruptions, first the call from Alonzo interrupted her television show planning, and then the call from her renter interrupted the renovation planning. And then as soon as Mitzy was back at her desk, the phone rang again.

The station manager had called and begged her to fill in some empty time this afternoon. One of their advertisers had failed to pay and they were handling these situations with no mercy. Everyone seemed to love Johnny and Mitzy spots so it seemed a perfect quick fix if she could be had on short notice.

Johnny at the radio station was cute, but he was so crass. Mitzy didn't mind flirting, or rather, she was a natural at it. But Johnny had a way of making her think she had gone too far. She wondered if it was just his radio personality. The whole flirting with her thing might just be his radio personality as well. He might not have two thoughts about her in real life.

She watched him through the window into his booth as he chatted with the weather and traffic guy. It would just be really nice to have someone to bring to the Dinner with Degas. Really, really nice.

Don't be unequally yoked... The old advice nagged at her. When it came to that she couldn't think of a single man that was her equal. She was either too old or too young, or too busy and too independent for most men she met.

She turned and looked at her reflection in the hall mirror. She didn't look bad, either. She sighed. She didn't think of herself as vain, but she did dress well for work. She had on her favorite purple business suit. It was the kind with a fitted jacket that skimmed the top of her low rise slacks. She had a shiny tank under her jacket. She felt very hip in this suit. Her hair was a good three inches up off her forehead, curls perfect, and not stiff. Her make-up, understated. She took a deep breath and stood up tall. She'd ask him to the dinner today or she'd never ask him. She thought about her ratings. Definitely, if she asked him at all, it would be while on air. People loved a private romance gone public.

She turned to his window again. It would be so much nicer if she knew he was a Christian man.

The producer nodded through the window, she opened the door, and went in.

"Hey, baby, in for a nooner?" Johnny winked and pushed a chair out for her.

Foreclosed

Her stomach fell down to her knees and her face fell too. She didn't want to go out with a man who thought that was funny.

She sat down. "In what world would you think that was an appropriate thing to say to a friend and a colleague?" Her voice was warm with hurt and disappointment.

"A man can dream, Mitz, a man can dream." Johnny smirked at her and winked again. "And if I'm dreaming about you, it isn't my fault. You look fine this afternoon. Who put that smile on your face, if you didn't get it looking forward to seeing me?"

"Where is your brain today, Johnny? Your radio station is going broke and begging people to sit here and talk to you. You think I'm smiling because you made a rude pass? My livelihood isn't dependent on what your listeners think of me." Mitzy looked over at the producer. The producer shrugged. "You, however, have to come here everyday and talk to the kind of people who want conservative news, financial reports, and a traffic update. They want Dr. Laura for Pete's sake. If you want people to pay their hard earned dollars advertising on your station you had better give a little thought to the kind of chatter you fill the air with. You don't want to be the reason people tune out for good."

"No, I was wrong. That's not a smile and you haven't been getting lucky. But how that long pole got all the way up—"

"That's it, Johnny. You've lost the Neuhaus morning spot. You can explain it to the station manager." She threw her headphones down and stormed out of the booth.

36

By the time she hit the hall tears were stinging her eyes. How dare he? How *dare* he!

Things were starting to come apart. Quitting her radio spot on the air in a hissy fit for comments she could have handled on a day she hadn't wanted Johnny to be a nice guy—that wasn't her style.

Nonetheless, she left the radio station and drove all the way home. She was done with work for the day.

Alonzo lay in his hospital bed with a pounding head, tuned in to Johnny Headly's radio show. He had almost turned it off, when Mitzy joined him.

Mitzy was making herself out to be some kind of nun. He tried to picture her with her big hair and blue eye shadow dressed in a habit. His imagination rejected the long black robe. As much as he hated everything about her, he would hate to hide a good looking woman in a nun's habit.

But he shouldn't hate. He knew better. But was it okay to be incredibly aggravated by someone?

Alonzo got to thinking about his property issues again. He ought to get out of his little dump of an office, throw some paint on it, and get someone else in it.

And then what?

He really wanted an acre or so in the downtown industrial area. He was serious business and that's where serious business went on. Sure, the

Eastside had an industrial area, but it wasn't the same. So why even bother with that dump of Neuhaus'?

He tallied its benefits. Location, location, location.

The commercial lumberyard. The stoneworks. The railroad. And if you can't be on the Westside at least you can be right by the river on the Eastside.

The area would probably gentrify in the next couple of years as well. Perfect really. A few million dollar lofts and some money yuppies on the street—those were the kind of people he wanted walking past his Miramontes sign every day. Exactly the kind.

The thing was, there wasn't a single building that size available for five miles in either direction. Everything was let already. The location was happening.

Caution told him he could bide his time and someone was sure to go out of business and vacate. But he wanted to fill his time, not bide it. He wanted to buy a property, fix it to suit and get a little renter in his hole of a place to increase his cash flow. Simple.

Mitzy was really pissed off—er—peeved off by that radio guy, and he was stuck in the hospital until later that evening. So he sat and listened to Johnny Headly throw his radio career down the toilet by talking smack about women in general right before the Dr. Laura show. *Why were people always so stupid?* he wondered.

Mitzy laid her head on her pillow, her grandma's afghan tucked up under her chin. She wished she had the energy to make a cappuccino. She wished she had someone to call.

Without a successful radio spot her hopes of getting on *First Things* were gone. She didn't want to go to the gala fundraiser without a date. But the Dinner with Degas was her one chance to meet new people who might want to buy a mansion. She really wanted a buyer for the mansion. It would help the guys at the stoneworks. It would help that poor Laurence Mills who was getting foreclosed. It would perk up her staff considerably.

Her staff.

She sighed. She could always take Ben. His girlfriend wouldn't mind. His girlfriend was twenty-two and very secure in her adorableness. Mitzy hated to take a kid like Ben to an event. It would make her look…was she too young to be a cougar?

She buried her face. She had everything except a few rather important things, like a best friend, or a fella. Or at this moment, a satisfying and fulfilling career.

After a good long sulk she washed her face and changed her clothes. She had dinner with her sister-in-law to contend with still.

Foreclosed

Chapter Three

Dinner at Brett and Aerin's. Never the most fun, but it had to be endured if Mitzy wanted the tickets to Dinner with Degas. She'd talk to Ben about the event the next morning. At least he made clever conversation.

Aerin wasn't one to beat around the bush. "Be sure to get these to Mother in time for her to make her hair appointments and get a dress." She slipped an envelope into Mitzy's purse.

"Did you get an extra set for my parents this year?" Mitzy tried to sound natural as she asked. Altering their firm but unspoken routine would be tricky.

"Of course not. I get very few comp tickets. The rest go for hundreds of dollars each." Aerin stared at Mitzy. "Why would you think I have an extra set?"

"Well…I assumed as you wanted me to get some tickets to Mom, you must have had two sets. You're always so kind to give me tickets every year. And I always make a donation…" She had to mention the donations. She just had to. Her parents weren't museum members. They never donated more than ten dollars at the event.

But Mitzy did. However much Aerin and Brett chose to disdain her career, the board of directors was always happy with her donations. Especially last year's gift.

"Oh. I see."

Last year Neuhaus New Homes had given the largest donation at the gala event. It was a small year in general, but that had made Mitzy's donation stand out all the more. There was some talk of a plaque on the wall.

"You know, Mitzy, if you are thinking of our little foundation, you might actually think of hosting your own table this year."

It was a risky move for Aerin to say that. She had no wish at all for a table full of trashy Southeast Portland Realtors and their friends in construction. She held her breath, hoping that her sister-in-law's business was too strapped by the economy to put up the five thousand dollars required to sponsor a table at the year's largest arts fundraiser.

Mitzy smiled brightly, honestly pleased. She had been asking for four years for particulars on how to host a table. Four years. And every year she was put off with the same comp tickets that she was expected to give to her parents. "Oh, Aerin, that would be perfect. Here's my card. Please have your office call my assistant and we will put it together immediately. I'm sorry there are still tables available at this late a date, but I'm so glad that I can host one!"

Aerin's lips disappeared in a tight knot. Her nostrils flared. "Oh, darling, I just mean I think we can fit something in for you, at the last minute." She waved her hand towards the kitchen. "Must go check dinner."

At the dinner table Mitzy kept the conversation on food. In the early days, when Aerin was a grad student and Mitzy was still in high school, they had bonded—a little—over food.

"This is terrific. Panko breading, right?"

"Absolutely. And I went to the Euro grocery downtown for the proscuitto. It cost an arm and a leg, but so much better than what you get from Trader Joe's. It's imported from Florence."

"I think Trader Joe's comes from Milwaukee." They both laughed. Despite what seemed like easy conversation, it was taking all of Mitzy's concentration to keep the mood light. She could see the steel in Aerin's eyes.

Brett was a lawyer and very used to tense situations. He was also used to tense situations between his wife and his sister. And frankly, he didn't care. For one thing, the Mariners were playing and he had ordered the game on pay-per-view. If he could eat whatever the muck on his plate was, panko breading or not, in fifteen minutes he could be back to the TV before the last inning was over.

Neither of these two women cared about sports. Let them have their panko breading. He wasn't going to pause to talk; he was going to eat. The other thing on his mind was even more important than baseball, but he wanted to get away from the bickering to think about it.

Foreclosed

"Are the beans from your garden?" It might have been odd in some place like New York, but in Portland, a flourishing garden was a sign of upper class green-mindedness. This year Aerin had turned her front yard into a vegetable garden.

She had even been featured in Better Homes and Gardens. Aerin and Brett were both very proud.

Aerin had offered the photographer a show in the modern gallery at the museum. Ostensibly it was because she was so impressed by his skill, but Mitzy was fairly certain it was to keep connected with a man who could get her press. The value of good press was another area on which Mitzy and Aerin could agree, if only Aerin would admit it.

"They are. Aren't they divine? There is nothing as earthy and satisfying as home grown beans. Of course these were frozen from last year, but I think they kept really well." Preserving the fruits of your garden was equally in vogue right now.

"They really are divine. I still have a gallon bag left. I'm saving them—I don't know exactly why, I'd just hate to be completely out!" Aerin was very good at the things she chose to do—fundraise for the arts, go green, or ruin an evening with her icy demeanor.

"You ought to use them, Mitzy, they won't keep forever." It was the way she said 'Mitzy'—as though Mitzy really were too stupid to know when to eat food—that put the chill on the table again.

After her disappointment at the radio station, Mitzy couldn't keep nice, not for another minute. She smiled sharply (regretting it even as she spoke). "Did I hear that your corporate sponsor backed out of the gala this year?"

Brett's head popped up from his speed eating.

Aerin almost dropped her fork. "We did have a last minute cancellation, yes."

"Have you found a last minute replacement yet? I have a few ideas if you have run out of people to call." Mitzy knew she should stop. She was not being gracious or kind. She was picking at a sore spot to make Aerin mad.

"We have, in the past, allowed certain organizations hosting rights to the whole dinner. This year, the people we expected to be most interested in our Dinner with Degas theme were not able to handle the expense of hosting. Having hosting rights is a very valuable position for businesses, but not something we rely on, or...even prefer. We prefer the art to speak for itself."

Confirmed.

That was the snippet of conversation Mitzy had overheard. They had no 'host' for the event. If she remembered, hosting the event came in well above fifty thousand dollars last year. But this year...and at the last minute...Mitzy made a few mental notes to share with Sabrina.

Aerin was important and powerful actually, at the biggest museum in their rather large town. But no matter which way she styled herself, she was not the Director of Development. Aerin may not love the top of mind factor Neuhaus had in real estate on the Eastside, but Mitzy thought the Director of Development wouldn't be so fussy about where the money came from.

Mitzy could get in at a large discount, she was fairly certain. And Dinner with Degas, by Neuhaus New Homes would give Mitzy the right polish for selling the Victorian. She might not make back her costs in the commission from the house, but there would be future work. And she always welcomed a tax deduction.

Brett returned to his game and Mitzy and Aerin felt no need to keep up the pretense. As soon as Brett left the table, Aerin took her plate to the kitchen and stayed there. Mitzy let herself out.

Early in the morning, a few days later, Sabrina braved the light rain to take another peek at the Baltimore place. She wanted to see if the bank signs had gone up yet. Its status on the county GIS hadn't changed, so she didn't know who was handling the foreclosure. She had very few things on her to do list, and even fewer that were as interesting as spying out this house.

This time, she didn't care at all about appearances and pulled a rugged little step ladder along with her. She set it up under the kitchen window and climbed on up. She leaned in close to the window and cupped her hands around her eyes. The morning was dim and gray and she wasn't seeing clearly. She couldn't be seeing clearly.

She squinted. She stared.

Her eyes weren't deceiving her.

It was all gone!

Sabrina took some pictures with her phone and moved on to the next window. There seemed to be a built-in display or hutch but it was in pieces on the floor.

She made her way around the house, peering closely into all of the downstairs windows. She took a couple more pictures, but nothing seemed as exciting as the kitchen, though wires hanging in the front room seemed to indicate a missing light fixture. And there was a hole, or some other sort of damage to the far wall in one of the rooms. The light was getting dimmer as the rain clouds rolled in and she couldn't tell if everything she was seeing was newsworthy.

She packed up her phone and her ladder and made her way back to the office. She'd beat Mitzy in this morning. And with news to share.

But Sabrina didn't beat Mitzy in. Mitzy was in the bull pen, nursing a coffee and looking glum.

Mitzy never looked glum. Sabrina dropped her bag and went to her friend.

"What's wrong?"

"Ben is going out of town the only weekend I actually need him around." She rested her head on her hand.

The event hosting had been arranged, for a song, really, but she couldn't see the good of the name recognition. Not without being there in person to meet the people, shake their hands, build connections with them.

She had skipped getting her own table and gotten herself a seat with the board of directors by her donation.

Make that two seats.

And she had no one to sit with. It was unendurable and yet she knew it shouldn't be.

"Um…so?" Sabrina hadn't been let into the date dilemma. She knew nothing of her boss's disappointment at the radio station. She knew nothing of Mitzy's bitter little attack on Aerin over dinner.

She did know that Dinner with Degas for Portland Arts Council was now Dinner with Degas by Neuhaus New Homes for Portland Arts Council. But that was all.

Mitzy sighed, and then looked up at her friend. "So now I have no one to take to the event. I don't know why this is getting me down, I really don't. But I finally have our name on this event. It is exactly the right venue to get a new line of business, and I have two tickets. Two tickets to sit with the board of directors for the Arts Council. My brother will be there with his wife. My dad will be there with my mom. My employee has a life and I can't think of a single decent person to take to this event. Not one."

"What about your friend on the radio?"

Mitzy groaned. She rubbed her eyes, which felt old and tired. "I'll go, and you can come with me, Sabrina. Business as usual, me and my trusty assistant. It will be more fun with you than with someone I don't really like. You may be a girl, but you're nice to be around."

"That's a delightful idea. I'll get a pretty dress to match yours so we look cute for the Goings On section of the paper. But put the event out of your mind, I have some pictures to show you." While she was talking she plugged her phone into the computer and uploaded pictures of the Baltimore Victorian.

Mitzy saw what was wrong immediately. "You have got to be kidding me!" She stared at the empty kitchen in disbelief. Enlarged on the computer screen, it was clear that all the appliances and the counter were gone. In fact, it looked as though one or two of the cabinets were missing as well. "He did not strip the house. That lousy wretch! We are killing ourselves trying to sell this for him before he forecloses and he stripped the house. I cannot believe it."

"He doesn't actually know we are trying to sell the house for him," Sabrina said.

"That's no reason to strip the house. That beautiful kitchen—gone. It would have sold the home on its own. The quartz, that beautiful, beautiful quartz."

Mitzy's cell phone rang.

"Yes? You know what, I will. I will let him apologize. I'll be right there." She hung up the phone and grabbed her purple croc Birken bag. "I'm going to the radio station."

Foreclosed

She sat in the radio booth with the station manager and a very contrite Johnny Headly.

Before Johnny could read his statement about family friendly radio and respecting women as equals, Mitzy leaned into her microphone and spoke. "I'm sorry, Johnny. I wasn't very friendly the other day."

Johnny's eyes narrowed suspiciously.

"For a couple of years now I have let you talk to me like we were in junior high. What I should have done was spoken with you privately about how that kind of joking around made me uncomfortable and was probably not what your audience wanted to listen to. I know that you are pretty new to talk radio. Things are different when you are a DJ. But it was wrong of me to lash out at you on air." Her voice was warm and sincere, but her stomach was in knots. Apologizing on air was the most humiliating thing she had done since junior high school. But she meant every word of it.

Johnny croaked and the manager stood, shaking his head. Johnny finally turned on his microphone. "How do you do it, Mitzy? I was a complete jerk to you on the radio. You gave me what I deserved. We begged you to come here and give us a second chance, and you out class me again. Really, how do you do it?"

She looked over at the station manager with a question on her face. They went to church together. He nodded to her. "Do you really want to know why?"

"I'm dying to know why."

"If I have any class at all, it's from Jesus, my friend. That's all there is to it. On my own I'm just as bad as anyone else, as you well know. You ought to be mad at me for leading you on!" Mitzy caught his eye and smiled.

"Yeah, I ought to."

The sick feeling in Mitzy's stomach hadn't gone away yet, so she kept going. "You may have noticed that I can talk. I can talk and talk. And being a talker has gotten me in trouble more than once. Especially when I'm mad. Just the other night at dinner I was so rude to my sister-in-law it was almost unpardonable. I picked and picked at her until she just got up and left."

"That can't be true, baby. Look at you, all class and Jesus. There's no way you did that. She probably deserved it."

"Come on. Really? Who deserves that? No one deserves to have a dinner guest come over and pick at you all night long. I was just awful. But when I'm mad, I'm mad. God has to change it; I can't change it myself."

"Are you mad now?"

"Funny you should ask. I am so mad I could spit nails right now."

"What has gotten Miss Mitzy Neuhaus so hot and bothered?" He was leering a little again. Mitzy raised her eyebrow at him.

"I mean, what has gotten under Mitzy Neuhaus' skin?"

"Property theft."

"Hot dang. Were you robbed?"

"Kind of. And you were kind of robbed. And frankly we were all kind of robbed. But mostly one bank or another was robbed. Tell me, Johnny. When you lose your house, who owns it?"

"Do you know something I don't know?"

"Come on, play along. Say you went into foreclosure. Who owns the house?"

"The bank, I guess." Johnny tipped back in his chair.

"That's right, the bank. They own the house. The whole house. You can't sneak back into the house you just lost and steal the built-in china cabinet, the river rock fireplace and five hundred feet of the floor plan."

"Well, now, obviously you can't. That's physically impossible, Mitz."

"Yes. And you can't steal the kitchen either." Mitzy bounced in her chair. Her heart was pumping. Everyone (who listened to AM radio) was going to hear about the crime at her dream house. She was going to make a real difference. And the she was going to catch the guy who stole the kitchen.

"Also physically impossible—wait. Not entirely."

"That's right. Kitchens are sort of portable." Mitzy grinned. "But they are definitely property of the owner of the home. If you sell the home and write into the contract that the refrigerator, stove, etc. are included, then they are included. But the kitchen counter tops? If they exist at the time the contract is written, they stay with the house."

"Of course."

"But if you lose your home you lose your kitchen. You lose the appliances and the really expensive quartz countertop, you lose the house.

It is really sad." Mitzy rocked back in her chair. It tipped a little too far. She caught herself and laughed.

"Slow down, sister, you're getting all worked up."

"Sorry! I'll try and be good. Here's the thing, somewhere, while you are wrestling with the bank and trying to save your home, there might actually be a Realtor trying to sell it as well. We notice empty homes. We try to connect people with them. But if the owner sneaks in and strips the stuff that could help us sell the house you totally ruin our chances of negotiating a great deal for you that might actually save your credit—and your future! It is maddening."

"Are you saying Realtors are economic superheroes?"

"I am anyway!" Mitzy's feet were tapping the floor a mile a minute.

Johnny reached over and tapped her knee. Then he put his finger to his lips.

Mitzy made a silent apology and tried to keep her feet quiet.

"You take this real estate thing pretty seriously."

Mitzy took a deep breath and tried to keep her voice calm. "Of course I do. These are homes where people live and build their lives. They are investments that make people's futures secure. They aren't just Jenga blocks to be slipped out bit by bit, loser makes it crash. It's ridiculous."

"Call me psychic, Mitzy, but I think you have a certain property in mind."

"It's true. There's a house I absolutely love. It's a huge historic home in Southeast. I've been working the system every direction to make a connection with the right buyer. I've been sad for the owner who is losing his home. I've been sad for the neighbors who have a vacant place on their street. I've been heartbroken for my friends, who remodeled the kitchen and were never paid. It makes me sick that some unknown person ripped the kitchen out."

"I've been doing a little Googling while you talked. Did you know that it really is stealing? It's a jail time crime."

"It ought to be."

"It is."

"Then I am going to pin this guy down. I'm going to sell that house and pin the guy down. He can't get away with this. The house is too important to be treated the way he did. It will have the right owner and he will get put away for what he did."

"You get 'em, tiger."

Johnny and Mitzy smiled at each other in conspiracy. *At least he didn't call me cougar*, she thought.

Laurence Mills was listening to the radio as he ate his lunch in his pickup. *Did Mitzy Neuhaus just say quartz countertop?* He turned it up and hunched forward over his wheel. He heard everything she said. Every threat she made. He revved his engine and hit the road running.

Chapter Four

At the office the following morning, Mitzy and Sabrina pored over their respective computers.

Sabrina hunted Craigslist for new listings of high end appliances for sale.

Mitzy looked for any personal information regarding Laurence Mills. She wasn't above hiring a private detective, but she sure would prefer to do it all herself. However, she was getting nowhere.

"After your radio show yesterday, I'd bet his postings have been pulled," Ben said from his desk, where he had nothing in particular to do. Parts of a paperclip and rubber band crossbow were spread across his desk. His feet were up on the garbage can. His back had been up since Mitzy didn't offer him a spy job. "It's because I was with Jenny this weekend wasn't it?" he muttered.

Foreclosed

The phone rang and Ben answered it. "Yes? Really? Just a moment." Ben spun around in his chair, kicking the garbage can over. "Is there a Realtor in the house, gang? A home just sold!"

Sabrina dropped her coffee. "Don't holler!" Sabrina patted her dress dry with the mouse pad.

Mitzy was already on the phone. "Yes? The property on 72nd? Umm hmm. Yes, it is a beautiful home. No, it's not a short sale. Absolutely that's the price. It's a great deal, isn't it? No, I swear it's not a short sale. Standard closing in thirty days. Just fax over the offer, okay? Who do they want to underwrite it? Really? You're kidding, then we can probably close much sooner. Okay. Fax over the offer. I'll get my seller on the phone. Thanks."

She looked at her colleagues, complete surprise written on her face. "A cash buyer, I must be dreaming. It had better be a good offer. The Smythes have been waiting forever and the price is so low they just can't take anything else off."

The three anxious real estate professionals sat with their eyes fixed on the fax. They were about to give up when it started spitting papers onto the floor. Mitzy scooped them up and passed them on after she scanned them.

"No kidding," Ben said.

"No kidding," Mitzy agreed.

"That's a great offer. The Smythes had better take it."

"Why wouldn't they? It's almost full price, buyer to pay all the closing, just like in the olden days. Okay guys, I'm off to bring some very happy news to our friends on 72nd Street." Mitzy slipped into the private office to make the call.

The Smythes accepted the offer and Mitzy called the other Realtor back to tell her. They arranged a bank to meet at to make the purchase. They would do the transaction tomorrow.

She came out of the little office, a happy, hopeful smile on her face. The sale helped soothe the sting of losing the great kitchen in the mansion. "Ben, get a welcome home package together. We have some friends closing tomorrow."

Ben flipped a pencil off the edge of his desk. Sabrina cheered.

If Ben had been a girl, they would have had a group hug.

Sabrina and Mitzy exchanged a meaningful glance. With a grin, from ear to ear, Mitzy called Joan.

The three ladies met down the block at a little coffee shop for a quick celebration.

Ben stayed behind to work on his welcome basket. It was boring and effeminate, but it was better than playing addictinggames.com for another day in a row.

Mitzy's table was covered with grande non-fat lattes and a sampler platter of pastries.

"It is exciting, but it's a little odd, isn't it? How many cash sales do you guys do a year?" Joan sipped her coffee.

Foreclosed

"A year? I don't think there is a yearly. In the last five years we may possibly have done three. So I guess it is unusual, but unusual in a good way. We need a closing. For morale." Mitzy held her cup close to her mouth and blew into it. Everything about the industry was unusual right now. Cash buyers were everywhere—at short sales and auctions, but this kind of full price family home buyer was a welcome oddity.

"It's great news, Joan. Don't be a downer. The 72nd house is a lovely home." Sabrina didn't want Joan to ruin the one piece of good news Mitzy had had in days.

"She's right, Sabrina. It is unusual. I know. But I don't want to think about that. The buyer's Realtor says they are good for it. They are going to the bank together to do the transfer in person. I don't see how it could go wrong." In reality she saw quite a few ways it could go wrong, but didn't feel the need to share.

"But the 72nd property isn't anything special. If you could lay down cash wouldn't you do a custom home, or a great location, or a vintage property?" Joan was persistent.

"We might do that. But we are single business women. The 72nd house is in an incredible school district. It is immaculate and has had all the green efficiency upgrades. You know, I bet it's a property firm. I bet someone is buying it as an investment. In fact, I really would bet. A lot of people are losing really nice homes in the crash. They need someplace to live. And even if they have to rent they want to rent something comparable to what they lost." Talking it through was increasing Mitzy's confidence. That house was a sound investment. Of course it was a property management company.

"Okay, let's bet. Dinner at Nero's on the loser."

"You're on." Joan and Mitzy shook on it.

They chattered over their coffee. They hadn't had the excitement of a sale in weeks.

Ben hit print and stared out the window. A mild looking man of middle height walked past. His jacket was tan. Totally nondescript. Ben laughed at himself. He described the nondescript guy.

A teenage girl on a bike rode past without a helmet. Idiot. She'd get herself killed in this traffic.

Two old men cut through the parking lot. They would probably be headed for a bench on the river. The nondescript guy came back this way and stopped at Bean Me Up Scotty's.

The women folk weren't hurrying back. Ben laid the welcome home package on Mitzy's desk for her to sign. He shuffled through the gift card drawer and pulled out a few for her to choose from. He had already ordered the flowers. He checked his watch. 10:30. Not even time for lunch yet.

Another teenager, this one on a skateboard and male, rode past.

A guy on a scooter slipped through traffic, apparently also wanting to get killed.

Another guy in a tan jacket was across the street looking in windows.

Foreclosed

Or was it the same guy?

Maybe that's why nondescript had come to mind earlier. He really had no idea if this was the same guy or not.

He looked out the side window…no one there. This guy entered the café, so he must not have been the same man. But then, who buys a coffee at a little hut and then goes to a café?

Ben shuffled through his desk drawer looking for something that needed to be done. Nothing came up so he opened up his games file and made ready to sweep for mines. "Kill me now," he said aloud to himself.

The nondescript man in the tan jacket watched the tall blonde at the table with her friends. She was in profile and arguing something with energy. He pulled his phone out of his pocket and took three or four pictures of the scene, then quietly entered the café. He ordered a coffee and took his seat at the table, directly behind the blond woman.

"Seriously, Joan, in what world was Clamato juice ever a good idea?" Sabrina was vehement.

"It was a different generation. They spiked it. It's good." Joan tried to defend her weakness for tomato and clam juice.

"Something's fishy about Clamato juice," Sabrina said with a straight face.

Mitzy snorted. "I bet you drink your Clamato juice with tomato aspic."

"Give me some credit, please," said Joan pulling a long face.

"Tomato is a fruit. Fruit Jell-O is classic."

"With celery and olives!" Sabrina threw in.

"What was the worst food you've ever had at an open house?" Mitzy asked Joan.

"Oh the worst? Goodness, mostly it's just stale cookies and burnt coffee. But once someone tried to serve homemade tiramisu at an open house. It smelled like a cheap bar in the house and the carpet was almost ruined from where bits of it dropped as people toured. It tasted good, but it was really a disaster."

"I once showed a home right after the family had spent the day making homemade sauerkraut." Mitzy attempted to suppress a laugh, but failed. Her head was light and everything was funny, like she had sucked on a helium balloon. She took a deep breath to pull herself together, but even that made her laugh.

Sabrina hiccoughed and her bobbed brown hair swung around her face as she rocked with laughter.

Joan leaned back in her chair and looked at them over the tops of her granny glasses. "You children need to pull yourselves together."

Something rustled loudly behind Mitzy. She turned around and saw a large newspaper open in front of a man in khaki pants. "Sorry if we're disturbing you." Her voice was low and serious which sent Joan into a wheezing laugh, for reasons she couldn't have explained.

Foreclosed

The man lowered his newspaper and looked Mitzy up and down. "Not at all," he said.

Mitzy thought it sounded as though he had a bit of an accent. English maybe? His paper went up with a loud rustle before she could ask him where he was from. He didn't look foreign…or maybe he did. She couldn't quite remember what he looked like. Sort of nondescript.

However little they may have been disturbing him, they had been disturbed and turned back to their coffee more subdued.

"Speaking of fishy, I still think paying cash for the 72nd house is a strange move. Very strange." Joan took a slow sip of her coffee and looked at her young friends over the tops of her glasses.

"So what?" said Sabrina.

"So…what if it is some kind of cover? Money laundering, for example."

"Again, so what? We couldn't prevent it and it wouldn't harm us," Sabrina said.

"Doesn't crime harm us all? And the amount of money we are talking about…well…we could talk to a few people if we honestly thought there was something wrong with the transaction. Why couldn't we? What are Attorney Generals for? Or is that District Attorneys? We could talk to my brother, actually, if we felt like we needed legal advice. Which I don't feel. We do cash transactions sometimes." Mitzy was torn between supporting the absolute right and closing her eyes with the hope that the sale was completely legit.

"Money laundering was just one thing it could be. It could be identity theft," Joan said.

"How on earth could it be identity theft?" Sabrina asked

"Apparently Sabrina has left her imagination at the door. Someone could have stolen an identity and be clearing out that bank account by buying a house for cash." Joan lifted an eyebrow. She seemed to be enjoying her theories now.

"That would leave one easy to follow paper trail. Do you realize how many places those forms have to be signed and how quickly the person would realize that their hundreds of thousands of dollars were gone? The house would immediately go back to the bank. The bank would have to pay all of the money back. The person trying to perpetrate the crime would be snapped up—there are cameras all over banks. We would know exactly what the person looked like. Ridiculous." The women sat in silence for just a moment. It was just long enough for Mitzy to wonder again what the man sitting behind her looked like. But when she turned to peek, the chair behind her was empty.

They brought the remains of the pastry feast to the office with them. "Thanks a million," said Ben, helping himself to a bear claw.

"Any calls?" Mitzy asked.

"Nope," Ben said.

"Good package, thanks," Mitzy said, flipping through the papers on her desk. "Why don't you take tomorrow off, Ben? Things are awfully quiet."

"Thanks, Mitz. I could use it. Is there anything at all I can do for you guys today?"

"You could run to the dry cleaners and pick up the order for *Homes by Joan*," Joan offered.

Ben looked up at Mitzy with one eyebrow lifted.

"If you want." She looked at her watch. "Okay, Ben, go pick up the drapes and things for Joan and then take the rest of the day off as well as tomorrow. Consider yourself on call and if something urgent comes up be ready to save the day, okay?"

Ben's shoulders relaxed. "I can do that. Thanks." He grabbed the drycleaners slip from Joan and made his way out.

"One sale is great, but it's just not enough. Sabrina, go ahead and get back on the *First Things* proposal. Joan, stay, go, whatever. Your call." Mitzy waved her hand behind her as she sat down to her desk as though to say, 'The world is your oyster.'

Chapter Five

Alonzo had been back at work for two days, if you could call it work. Yesterday he had put his staff into rolling lay offs. It made his gut feel like it was filled with rocks to do it, but there was no work coming in.

No money.

If they could all take a bit of the hit, they could all stay for the long haul.

He had one large emergency savings. He tossed around ways he could use his life savings to save his company, but nothing he came up with was big enough to get them through an endless economic depression.

He did have one idea that would help his business in the short term, and his family in the long run.

Foreclosed

He called his sister. "Hey, sis. I got a proposition for you. Sit down and don't get all noisy until I'm done. Diego still out of work, right?" His brother-in-law was a roofer, residential. "Yeah, yeah, I know. Business is bad everywhere. But I have an idea for you. You want to run a business?" He listened to his sister explain that running her home was a business and that she was working besides as a tutor at Diego Jr.'s school and on and on. "Alright, so you don't want to open an inn now? I thought you still wanted to." That quieted her down. "Yeah, that's right. My men need work. Your man needs work. Let's get going on the inn thing. I buy it, I renovate it—yes, yes, to your specs—and I'm a silent partner taking a cut on profit. We'll work out the papers with a real lawyer. Because I want it to succeed, that's why a real lawyer. Because you are a smart lady and will do a good job. Because I don't know anyone else I'd give my money to right now. Just you, sis. Okay. Okay. You go ahead and start looking. When you find the right place call me. Yes, you can buy a house. Well…no one has to know I worked on it. I'm kidding, calm down. Find the perfect old ratty house, we will fix it and make it a first rate destination. Good girl."

Carmella went on, effusively thanking him and giving quality time to her hard knocks for a bit longer before she let him go. Probably to call Ma and tell her all about it.

It was really a last ditch idea. He'd probably never see any of his money again. He might bankrupt himself, in fact. But it would keep his crew and their families fed for a while if the place she found was ratty enough.

He sat down at his desk to begin his plans. Rolling lay offs would probably go on for the next two months. Who could take the hit the best? He began to list his crew by age and family size so he could work out a pro rata that kept the most people fed the longest. In the back of his mind he wished that someone would make a list like this that included him. "God, just get us all through this," he mumbled as he wrote.

It hadn't been even an hour since Mitzy had sent Ben home for the day and she already had work for him. She received the specs for artwork they would need for the gala.

All Mitzy had to do was have her artist send the Neuhaus logos and artwork to the printers and the Arts Council would take care of the rest. She'd be meeting with the Director of Development to firm up the donation itself. In the meantime, and to show she meant business, she made an electronic deposit of the first $5000 at their website.

When Ben arrived with the drapes and other non-washables for Joan, Mitzy followed him to his desk, firing directions at him. "It has to be top notch, professional. This is a whole new clientele. I like what you do, Ben, I really do, but you have to work on a whole new level this time, and you only have until Monday to get it done. At that it's a rush job, the gala is on Friday evening. That is just not a lot of time."

Ben made a charade of consulting his completely empty schedule. "I think I can fit it in." In reality he was like a dog with a new bone. His energy was palpable. He had a real job to do and one that she wanted done well. His specialty.

Now that it was settled and really happening, Sabrina and Mitzy left to buy dresses.

"Going together?" Joan asked as she walked out with them.

"Yes." Mitzy sighed. Sabrina was fun, but it rankled to not have a date. It had been a while but she still remembered that real dates were fun.

"Well, there might be recently divorced, very rich men there. Try to dress like you are looking for men. You know, if you are."

Mitzy groaned. She took Sabrina's arm and veered away from Joan. She had to look like a woman with a mansion to sell. That was the goal of this event.

The next morning Ben had an impressive selection of artwork to choose from. It did his days at Rhode Island School of Design proud. But Mitzy was no closer to figuring out how to get her hands on Laurence Mills. During the night she had thought through her current goals:

1. Save the radio station, one Neuhaus New Homes segment at a time

2. Break into her television career

3. Survive a gala event

4. Find the perfect buyer for the Victorian (i.e. justice for James at Portland Granite and Stone)

5. Get Laurence Mills

'Get Laurence Mills' was the most exciting line item. Mills had begun to represent the unscrupulous, the criminal, and in general the element in society that caused the economic downturn in the first place. She had found herself unable to sleep these nights as she dreamed up ways of taking him to justice. By morning, her consuming vision was of this man shackled in an orange jumpsuit facing the judge. He'd get his. But how?

She nodded her head absently as Ben showed her his design concepts and explained the benefits of each. She pointed at the one with the lavender background. "That's fine." She was scribbling (literally) all over a legal pad, a thousand miles from the office.

"Are you sure? I mean, I like it. But it isn't the strongest of the designs. I think this one with the black borders has a more professional feel." Ben put the black bordered option on top.

"Oh, you're right." Mitzy kept scribbling.

"Hello—Mitzy? Are you there?" Sabrina waved a coffee in her boss's general direction.

"They're all fantastic, Ben. Give me ten minutes and then I'll pay attention and pick the best one. Sabrina, put the coffee down before you soak us all." She peeled her eyes off of her scribbled paper. "How are we going to catch this rat?" she said, through her clenched teeth.

Before anyone could give her a proper answer, the phone rang.

"Good morning, Neuhaus New Homes, this is Sabrina speaking, how can I help you?" Pause. "They haven't?" Pause. "Yes, I know. It's ten o'clock. Okay. I'll give her the message. Thank you." Sabrina hung up the phone.

"The buyer was a no show," she said, her voice full of disappointment.

"The cash buyer?" Ben asked.

"It's the only one we have. Or don't have," Sabrina replied.

"A no show? Really?" Mitzy sighed. She wanted to track down a criminal, not a lousy Realtor. "I'll call the buyer's rep and see what's going on." She pulled her phone out of the Birken bag and scrolled through the numbers. She hit send.

She waited.

"What?" She hung up and laid her phone on the desk. "It says the number has been disconnected. You have got to be kidding me." Mitzy's voice was clipped and strained.

"So it was all a hoax?" Ben asked.

"I have all the proper papers right here. I have the buyer's name, the Realtor's name and the contact number. I guess I'd better start calling around. This is not what I want to do today." Mitzy pulled a file folder off of the top of the 'active status' box and shuffled through her papers. She dialed 411 and began her contact number search.

"I knew that was too good to be true yesterday." Sabrina sighed into her coffee.

"Um, yeah, I think it was Joan who knew it was too good to be true," Ben said.

"Even if I didn't say it, it felt too good to be true. No one has cash anymore. We won't see cash again this decade." Sabrina had been hopeful yesterday and today was back down in the dumps with the rest of the world.

"Mitzy has cash," Ben said.

"Mitzy is smart. No one else has cash. You don't have cash," Sabrina said.

"Neither do you." Ben turned back to his computer.

"Duh. Of course not. Only Mitzy does. I'm going to see if the Victorian is listed yet." She booted up her computer and logged onto the multiple listing service. "Here it is, guys. Listed for almost one hundred thousand less than Mr. Mills bought it for."

"The bank deserves to take the hit. So I didn't save it in time for the stoneworks guys? Foreclosed already?" Mitzy slumped a little in her chair.

"Foreclosed in a day? Never. It's listed as a potential short sale, upon bank's approval." Sabrina clicked through the photo tour as she talked. "It's in pretty rough shape. I wonder if anyone was even living in it."

"Short sale? Then it's not too late. A short sale makes it harder for me to get a solid offer on it. If I can find someone interested—if I make a good connection at the dinner, I might be able to approach the Realtor with it and get it unlisted, etc. I think we could make this still work. Complicated, yes, but possible. And speaking of Realtors, here is another listing for the 72nd house's buyer's rep. I think I'll try to reach her again." She picked up her phone and dialed the new number.

She got a voicemail. "Interesting. That's a home number, or maybe a cell. No mention of being a Realtor. Just the pre-recorded message—you know, that computer voice that comes with your phone." Mitzy tapped one manicured nail on her cell phone screen.

"That's not very professional. What do you think could be going on?" Sabrina was leaning back in her ergonomic chair, arms crossed over her chest.

"I think we were about to be conned, but the buyer chickened." Mitzy tapped her pencil on her legal pad full of scribbles. "It might be just what Joan was talking about yesterday. A potential identity theft situation but the criminal got scared. Or maybe it was some kind of money laundering but the boss found out. I don't know. But it seems like something wasn't right."

"It feels like anarchy in our industry right now. Thieves in the night, and everything," Sabrina said.

"Desperados," Ben volunteered.

"Thanks for that. But it does feel out of control. I bet the Realtor had one last chance and when the buyer was a no show, she just gave up. I hate to think of people quitting. It's not the time to quit; it's the time to keep moving forward. Keep trying. Keep active." Mitzy gazed out the front window of her quiet business office to the equally quiet street that was steel gray, with misty rain and looked like Disappointment Illustrated.

"Everybody buy war bonds. Uncle Sam wants you—to buy and sell Real Estate," Ben said.

"Sarcastic," said Sabrina.

"Let's not get down on each other, guys. We have work to do, real work. Ben, get back on the artwork, get all of the sizes and formats they requested ready and get our photos—all of us—over to the printer before lunch. Sabrina, have the proposal for the television show on my desk right after lunch—"

"No fair," Ben interjected.

"Ben."

"Just kidding."

"I am going to hit the road. I have a list of Victorians for sale in town—there are only five right now in the Eastside and none at all on the West. There is one in Northeast. I'm going to go visit them all and check them out. I'll see you both back here at two pm. Of course, if I sell a house while I'm out I'll call." Mitzy shrugged on her faithful purple blazer with the Neuhaus logo embroidered on the pocket and headed out. Research was legitimate busywork. She really just needed to get out of the office and be around houses for sale. It was almost as good as being around people buying houses.

She packed all of the folders from the active file into her Birken bag (a gift to herself after she had her first million dollar profit year) and left. The gray day was wet with spring rain, so she hit the road with her top up. She headed to her Victorian first.

"This is the one you want?" Alonzo asked his sister Carmella.

"Yes. It's perfect."

"How on earth is it perfect? It's a dump." He was completely unimpressed with the property she had brought him to. But he had been impressed by her quick decision making. Very rare. Apparently she had had her eye on it for a while.

"It has good bones, Al. It is the right size, plenty of bedrooms and room enough to add more baths. Can you imagine? A huge kitchen, a sun porch. It's still got an acre and a half of its own property."

"It's blocks off the main road, needs a complete renovation. It's nowhere near any tourist attractions. It is on a street of boring residential homes. Nothing about this place says bed and breakfast." Alonzo tromped through the muddy driveway. Working with his sister always gave him a headache.

"Do I have to spell it out for you, Alonzo? I can't believe you can't see this. First, it is set back a romantic distance from the street with a tree-lined roundabout drive. Second, there's room for a gazebo in the back and the property is edged on three sides with a bit of a forest for seclusion. And honestly did you not see what I saw when we turned on Baltimore?"

"Apparently not."

"Historic Old Church."

"Historic Old Church?"

"Yes."

He turned his head to the intersection of Baltimore and Smith Blvd. He could see the corner of the old stone building with its modest parking lot. He couldn't quite see the steeple because of the many trees. "Okay, what about the church?"

"Weddings. And wedding nights. I think all they do over there anymore are weddings and anniversary parties and that stuff. Maybe they have church there, I wouldn't know," Carmella said.

His mind was working quickly now. He bounded around to the back to view the property better. "You said there's a gazebo back here?" he hollered to his sister.

"What?"

"A gazebo?"

"What?"

"Get back here and talk to me!"

She huffed her way to the back of the property. "Yes. A gazebo back here. And we could trim up the trees. We could make this a real park back here."

"Yes. I see." He scanned the property making mental adjustments. "We could dig a pond right over there." He pointed off towards the corner of the lot.

"That would be fabulous. Now you are seeing it. You get married at Old Church and we can give you a discount on pictures in the back yard. Book your honeymoon night here and you can have the location for your photo sessions for free. We could even work out special deals with photographers," Carmella said.

"Brilliant." Alonzo pulled a notepad out of his pocket and began scribbling notes. "What's the asking price?"

Foreclosed

"That's the best part. It's a short sale. So…" She told him the price, a little red faced and embarrassed with pride. She knew it would seal the deal for him.

"Short sale. Hmmm." He wrote a few numbers down on his pad. "Short sale isn't good. It could take a year to get this going if we try to go a short sale. You know, this property is worth almost twice that price as a business. Let me check out the zoning and talk to the listing agent. We might be able to offer a price good enough to get moving on this faster." Alonzo heard a car pull up into the gravel drive. He paused, listening.

There was a big truck in the bucolic drive of the run down Victorian. That was slightly annoying to Mitzy. She supposed, being a listed property, other people could come see it now. But she had a mother hen attitude at the moment and wanted to cluck the weasel away from her nest. She sat in her Miata for a few minutes gathering her thoughts and prepping her reactions.

Mitzy caught sight of someone out of the corner of her eye.

She popped open the door of her car and climbed out.

Alonzo, though he knew who was getting out of the car, couldn't keep himself from admiring the long legs that stepped from it. He took a deep, admiring breath as the legs led up to…ah. That wretched purple blazer. The blazer in all the ads, the blazer that kept him awake at nights—or was that gave him nightmares? Whichever. It was the blazer of stereotype, the blazer with the big shoulder pads that went with the bouffant hair. And right above the shoulder pads was a pretty, but angry, face.

"Good morning, Mitzy." Alonzo forced himself to smile. The possibilities behind this coincidental meeting were not endless. She was probably the listing agent on the property. He was going to have to be nice.

"Mr. Miramontes," Mitzy said. She decided territorial was the best way to act right now. Make it a foregone conclusion that this was her property. "How can I help you?"

"Please, call me Alonzo. And this is my sister, Carmella." He indicated his sister who was peering into the front windows of the house.

Carmella was a statuesque brunette with hair piled on her head. Her jeans were tight and she was wearing heels. Mitzy decided not to analyze the relief she felt when he said sister. Though she suspected even if it was his sister she was probably also his type. Recognizing that for the very weird thought that it was, Mitzy tried to pull her mind back to the property.

"Carmella and I are interested in the property. Do you have some time to talk about it?" He leaned on the decrepit rail of the front porch, assuming nonchalance that none of them felt.

Mitzy squared her shoulders and stood tall. She was ready for conflict and not about to let her guard down to him—no matter how smoldering his eyes and deliciously thick and wavy his dark hair. The broad shoulders were—well—she wouldn't consider his shoulders at the moment. She didn't have time.

"That's nice of you to help your sister. Carmella, I'm Mitzy Neuhaus. How are you?" She smiled at the sister. Taking the business out of the hands of Miramontes seemed the right first move.

"Mitzy Neuhaus? *The* Mitzy Neuhaus? I love you! You were fabulous on the radio with that awful Johnny. Have you ever thought about getting your own show? It would be incredible."

Alonzo shuffled his feet and cleared his throat. Why did everyone who met Mitzy go into raptures like this? Ridiculous.

"I'm so glad this is your property, Mitzy. I've always wanted to meet you. What do you think of this house? It's amazing right? But what's your professional opinion?"

"It is a fantastic property, and really a steal right now." Mitzy tried to skirt around telling an actual lie. "It needs quite a bit of work though. Are you looking to move soon? I know of a few really great deals that are move-in ready."

"Oh no, I'm not moving. This is an investment." Carmella smiled at her brother, her face full of gratitude.

"It's quite a property to set up as a rental," Mitzy said. "I don't know if you could get enough in rent to take care of it properly. Not with all of this land."

Carmella laughed warmly. "Oh, it won't be a rental. It will be a business."

Mitzy made herself smile at Alonzo. "This is a residential property." She narrowed her eyes. "And I have an interested buyer already lined up."

All thoughts of skirting lies flew. This was her old money mansion, not a business investment for some Miramontes scheme.

Alonzo eyed her carefully. Mitzy wasn't confident. She was mad. Something wasn't entirely above board. He took a wild stab. "Residential, eh? It's zoned residential? Even with that church on the corner? And, what is that? He craned his neck to stare down to the end of the long street. "Isn't that an auto shop on the other end?"

"This is a family friendly street. Kids can ride bikes here. It's a terrible idea to turn this house into a business." Mitzy just barely kept herself from stamping her foot.

"Oh, but you'd like it. It's going to be a bed and breakfast!" Carmella's cheeks flushed and her eyes sparkled.

Mitzy took a deep breath. She did not want to make this worse my crushing Carmella's dream.

"You can't deny that it is a great location and building for a bed and breakfast." Alonzo walked over to Mitzy, and stood near her. He leaned close and said, "Isn't it romantic?"

Mitzy almost slapped him. She took three long steps backwards.

"Do you have an offer on the property or not?" Alonzo asked, switching his tone to business neutral.

Mitzy paused. "There isn't an offer as of yet."

"Then we will fax you the papers immediately." He almost turned to leave, when something on her face made him stop.

She chewed her bottom lip. She had to tell them.

"We should fax the papers to you, shouldn't we?" he asked with a sneer.

"Well…" She hesitated.

"I think we are done here." Alonzo walked purposefully to his pickup.

Carmella hurried after him.

They drove away, leaving Mitzy kicking herself for losing face. And possibly losing the house. The gala was coming quickly. There might still be time. She doubted, but she had to keep trying.

Alonzo tried to drive more carefully this time, even though he was mad. His neck was still sore from his recent accident, and he was in no mood to crash his pickup.

"Do you think we can still get the house? I mean, Mitzy is the best there is. I'm afraid if she doesn't want us to have it, we won't get it." Carmella chewed on the green coffee stirrer from her to go cup.

"It will be fine."

"Are you sure? I mean, she really is the best. If she thinks it's a bad spot for a business, maybe it is a bad spot for a business. Who else would know if not her?"

"She is not the best. She just advertises a lot." Alonzo gritted his teeth. He really felt like smashing something at the moment.

"Oh come on. I don't know what your problem is. She is too the best. Everybody knows her. Everybody sings her jingle. *When you need a new home, you can call Neuhaus, New Homes!* What's not to love? She's got kitsch factor like nobody."

"She's not kitschy. She's tasteless. She's just…she's just…annoying. She's really annoying." He braked hard at the light and regretted it as his head jerked forward.

"Calm down, big boy. She really gets your goat, doesn't she? No one else has a word to say against her. I'd have thought you'd love her, after all, she's a 'born again' like you." She laughed.

"So now all Christians are supposed to love each other, huh?"

"That is kind of the point." She laughed again and sipped her coffee.

He drove on in silence. Yes. It was true. It was kind of the point. But that didn't mean he had to like it.

Well, it sort of did.

"Let's get an offer on the Victorian this afternoon," he said after some moments of silence.

"I think I'll sleep on it. Never make a decision like this in less than twenty-four hours."

He pulled into his sister's driveway and let her out.

Yes, he'd have to work on being nicer to Mitzy if he wanted his family to recognize the Protestant thing he had going on. Not that he minded the Catholic Church he had grown up in, it just hadn't clicked with him the way this one did. And it would never click with his family if they didn't see him change.

He groaned. Why did this change have to start with that obnoxious girl?

Foreclosed

Chapter Six

Into every life eventually, a little laundry must fall. And that was how Mitzy was occupying herself when a most interesting fax came in. She couldn't hear the fax coming in the office from across the thirty-five hundred square feet of her penthouse. Especially not with the television on. It was quite a bit later, the next morning in fact, when she popped into her home office with her coffee, and saw the fax.

A little less than twelve months earlier, Mitzy had had Sabrina submit an application to appear on House Hunters. It was one of the many ways she had hoped to fill the time during the economic slump. Actually, the application process itself was the way she had hoped to fill the time. She had very little hope that the show would actually come to town this year. Though if they did, she fully expected they would call on her as the local agent.

Foreclosed

The fax was a formal letter, but had a personal note on the bottom. The letter said, generally speaking, that House Hunters would be filming in the Portland metro area in one month's time and that they were excited to be showcasing such a vibrant community. The note on the bottom was what really mattered. It was from Curt, Mitzy's one previous boyfriend—well—her one serious relationship at any rate. After things fizzled out he had remained friendly and then he had sort of disappeared. It was a nice note:

"Mitzy! I was totally amped to see your application! I'm insisting we work with you when we get to town. I'll be calling on Monday. Oh, by the way, I'm a producer for House Hunters now, go figure! – Curt"

She and Curt had broken up mostly over her career. Curt had been a camera man, a really good one. But Portland isn't known for its vibrant film and television industry. With her business thriving and her—Curt called it 'retentive'—sense of responsibility to her staff, things between Curt and herself just couldn't go anywhere. Make that, Mitzy wouldn't go anywhere, but Curt had to.

In fact, Mitzy had known that Curt worked for the show. It was her business to know HGTV as well as any other aspect of the real estate world, but she hadn't advertised the fact on her application. It seemed pointless. Ex-boyfriends aren't notoriously great references.

Mitzy laid the paper back on the fax tray and added House Hunters to her list of things to do. It seemed odd all of a sudden that last week was the slowest week of her business life, and this week she suddenly had too much to do. Today was Wednesday. She had less than a week to prep for the gala, get a television career, and catch a thief. If all things scheduled well, House Hunters would help with her media goals but if not…well…she wouldn't think about that right now. She had a dress in the closet, a fabulous proposal to *First Things* and a day to spend staking out the Victorian and hunting down Laurence Mills. The missing cash buyer came to mind. Probably nothing she could do about it at this point, but the Smythes deserved some kind of compassion right now, a phone call at the very least.

At the office, Ben was put on full time gala work. He was their liaison. He welcomed the break from monotony. He particularly enjoyed running around to the printers, whether or not he really had to, and seeing his work in production. He was out of the office, meeting with the boys at the print shop this particular morning.

Sabrina and Mitzy had the still office to themselves.

"I've been playing detective, boss," Sabrina said, pulling out a yellow legal pad.

"Oh?" Mitzy, reading glasses perched on her nose, was engrossed in her emails. She longed to be at the Victorian, but was a stickler about her business relationships.

Sabrina cleared her throat. "My friend at the DMV is having a hard time tracking down Laurence Mills."

"Excuse me?" Mitzy turned and gave Sabrina her full attention.

"Remember Ryan? We dated last year? He works at DMV still. I had him look up Laurence Mills."

"He can do that?" Mitzy asked, quite surprised.

"Sure. Apparently Hippa laws don't restrain the motor vehicle department employees."

"But he couldn't find anything?"

"Yes, but what he couldn't find was rather telling. In our state registry there are Laurie Mills, Laura Mills, Larry Mills, Lorenzo Mills, Lorent Mills and Florence Mills, but no Laurence. And Larry, Lorenzo and Lorent, the males, didn't even live in Portland, much less at our poor abused Victorian."

"So, it's a dead end."

"Kind of, but we now know he doesn't have a driver's license. Or at least a valid one. According to the tax record the Baltimore house was his address for most of this year and if he drives he should have a local license by now. I think it would be cool if Laurence Mills was a false identity."

"Very mature, Sabrina." Mitzy rolled her eyes.

"Maybe it's immature. But it's also more interesting."

"How would he buy a house with a fake identity?" Mitzy asked.

"You're the real estate expert, you tell me."

"He could use cash. If he didn't have to close at a title company, it might not be that hard." The lost cash buyer and their earlier hypothesis obviously came to mind.

"It could be possible." Sabrina smiled, pleased with herself.

"If we happened to be dealing with a person that didn't exist, how would we catch him?" Mitzy mused.

"We'd have to hunt him down all the same, I guess. I'd imagine if Laurence Mills wasn't really Laurence Mills that he'd been acting like Laurence Mills all the same. So maybe we don't change our method, we just add this tid-bit to what we know about him."

"Not bad, Sabrina. I'll keep this in mind. If we catch him and he isn't really himself we have more ways to get him in trouble." Mitzy grinned. She liked the idea of getting her kitchen thief in trouble.

"I'm going to go hang out around the house. Maybe visit Debbie at home, drink some tea and stare out her windows. I'd like to see if there are any comings or goings at the property," Mitzy said.

"You have a very nice tenant to let you drop by like that."

"I'm a lucky woman."

The gala was just two days away and Mitzy wanted to be secure on the status of the house before she found the perfect buyer—which was the whole goal of the gala after all.

It was a quiet visit. Debbie put on a pot of coffee and the two women stared out the window for hours on end, noting only one black pickup truck slow down as it passed the driveway. Was Laurence driving without a valid license and so adding to potential charges against him? Or was it just a curious person looking at the impressive old house? Mitzy noted the license plate number just the same. They could always run the numbers by the Old Boyfriend at the DMV.

Foreclosed

Chapter Seven

The Tiffany Center was an art deco building in the center of the downtown business district. It stood only five stories tall, but it was set up on the hill and made the most of what view it could manage. Through certain windows all you saw was the bustle of business in neighboring high rise buildings. The windows on the opposite side had peak-a-boo views of the river that reflected the sparkling lights of the multitude of cars commuting home across the bridges.

The interior had a deep, cozy feeling, despite the soaring ceilings and a twenty-five hundred person room capacity. The floors gleamed golden, the dais was set off by luxurious red velvet curtains.

A big band, with polished trumpets dancing and men in tail coats played on a stage set off to the side. The band leader was a dead ringer for

Foreclosed

Harry Connick Jr. and Mitzy had to look three times before she was sure it wasn't really him.

The room was filled with round tables. Each table was hosted by a contributor who either sold their seats for donations that covered the cost or invited potential donors to sit with them. Each table represented at least five thousand dollars, but potentially quite a bit more.

The prominent Dinner with Degas sign was flanked by the red velvet curtains. Chalk ballerinas stretched out their sketched legs behind the words. Hanging beneath that sign was Mitzy's.

The Neuhaus sign was a deep purple, almost eggplant, that complemented the red velvet curtain.

Her business name was a subtle, location inspired font—one might say Old Broadway or New York, New York writing. It said simply: Neuhaus New Homes Welcomes you to Dinner with Degas.

Each table had a similar sentiment written on coasters, cocktail napkins and a table tent. She had no idea how the printers had gotten all of that made in time, but she was very pleased with the effect it created. Her signage fit well in this posh setting.

For quite a while, she just stood back by a far table, admired the advertising and felt a bit overwhelmed by the luxury of it all. She knew it was going to be a gala affair, but she hadn't imagined how impressed she'd be by it.

Mitzy was wearing a classic little black dress. It was the 'When in Doubt' option. Her personal dresser at Saks was confident it was the correct choice. It was strapless, and draped to her feet, with a bit of a

Roman flair. So maybe it wasn't the 'little' black dress. But despite its length there wasn't much to it and she felt like a million dollars.

She had seen the stylist at Saks as well, just to pull her look together. They had tamed her riotous curls—a bit—and pulled them softly back at her neck. Stray curls, which she hadn't been allowed to mousse as usual, played around her face, giving her an altogether younger look than she had had in years.

Sabrina didn't have the same budget Mitzy had and wasn't willing to expense her look. However she had pulled herself together well enough in a simple, dark blue tea length number with a petticoat under and cap sleeves. Standing next to the Mitzy Neuhaus she looked exactly like what she was: a personal assistant and a poor substitute for a date. The impression she gave off, however, was of youth and humor and charm. In fact, when not standing beside her boss she was probably the prettiest and most comfortable of all the women in the room.

The low lights, candles on the tables, swinging big band music, and oversized reprints of Degas' favorite ballerinas made the two women feel like they had entered a wonderland. But only a few more moments passed before Howard Ruche, Director of Development for The Arts Council of Portland, which managed the fundraising side of the museum, found them.

He greeted them with his natural, bluff enthusiasm. "Well done, Neuhaus. Just look around at your magnificent event." He clapped them both on the back in a fatherly manner and began to maneuver them to the front of the ballroom.

Foreclosed

"No, Howard, you know we didn't do this. Your team did all of this," Mitzy said.

"We did it, but you believed that we could do something you'd be proud enough to put your name on and we can't thank you enough." A waiter in tails walked past, holding his tray of champagne high. Howard slipped two off of the tray and handed them to the ladies.

"It is my pleasure and responsibility this evening to ensure that you both thoroughly enjoy yourselves. Let me begin by introducing you to my lovely wife, Adele Ruche." A tall, thin woman, not much younger than Howard stood and allowed herself to be introduced. She handed Mitzy and Sabrina each a program.

"This looks to be a wonderful evening," she said with warmth.

Mitzy and Sabrina found their chairs at the table. Their table was to the left of the dais, in front of a large ballroom floor. "They've planned a lindy hop dance demonstration, followed by a bit of ballet. The ballet is for Degas, of course, but the swing sessions will be more fun. After that the ballerinas will come back out and do living dioramas of some of Degas' more famous pieces. Altogether it looks to be a more charming and entertaining event than last year's Evening with Andrew Wyeth. As theme's go, that wasn't much to work with. Beautiful pictures of course, but terrible as a theme."

"Why did they choose Wyeth if it was so difficult to plan the evening?" Mitzy understood how to sell a great house to a family, but convincing people to part with money for your cause was a bit bewildering.

"We try to plan our gala around the previous year's best new acquisition. The Wyeth piece was one the museum was rightfully proud of. But nabbing a Degas this year, well, it makes for a great gala, don't you think?"

"Absolutely." Mitzy digested the idea of combining your year's successes with a fundraising event. Of course your donors want to know you've been successful with their money. What a clever way to manage things. And really, not much different from hosting a well staged open house or home auction.

"Pardon me, ladies, there is someone here I need to greet personally. My nephew has come stag this evening. He's seated with us, so pardon the odd number at our table." She parted with the women and wandered off after her nephew.

Sabrina flipped through her program. "Ooh look, there's an auction. Hey bidda, bidda, bidda," she said.

"Hush, you'll get us kicked out." Mitzy hid a giggle behind her program. "Adele didn't mention an auction. I wonder if it's new for this evening's event. What page?" She opened her program and scanned the contents.

"Here, page eleven." Sabrina handed her program over.

"Jewelry? That's different." Mitzy sat upright in her chair. The very formal strapless gown didn't encourage slouching. She took a deep breath to relax a little and then read the small article about the jewelry holdings that were to be auctioned off.

Foreclosed

Across the ballroom Aerin tried to make conversation with her donors as they waited for the event to begin. She usually felt suave, sophisticated and rather young at this event. There was no getting around that those who support formal art museums like hers tended to be silver haired and hold family trusts. She was trying to keep engaged, but her eyes would keep straying to the head table where Mitzy sat as lovely as Psyche waiting for her Eros. It was unforgivable that she would be so perfectly put together tonight.

Everywhere Aerin looked she saw formal, attractive ads for what everyone knew was a plain old real estate office. And her sister-in-law who ought to hold stock in Aqua Net hair products and acrylic nails looked straight from the pages of Vogue.

Aerin herself had on last year's dress, which still fit fine. But the dress seemed less than sufficient now that everyone was gathered together. Soon her effusive parents-in-law would arrive. At the very least, it would take the pressure of conversation off of Aerin for a few moments.

Brett was lingering at the bar with a group of men and Adele, the boss's wife. Aerin recognized city council man Young, but not the other two men. She smiled broadly, her eyes crinkling charmingly at the elderly patron of the arts she was talking with. He was quite funny really, if she could just gather her thoughts and pay attention.

"My wife was put out altogether when she saw the auction. I'm afraid I'm going to have to buy the pendant back for her. Can you imagine what it will cost me to insure that rubbish?" he said gruffly, but with a twinkle in his black eyes.

"Pendant, I'm sorry, what do you mean buy her back the pendant?"

"Way back in nineteen twenty-seven, her father donated some old family relics to the museum. The museum was just getting up a jewelry collection. Prosperity, jazz music, rail roads, all that rot. Not that I remember of course, I was just a baby back then." He tapped the floor with his wooden cane. "Everyone was rich, everything was beautiful, and everything had to be new. So her father donated some old Russian relics that had been his mothers, Romanov, I think, to the museum. The revolution was old news you know, it had been ten years or so and everyone forgot how much they used to love poor Alexandria and her girls. Well anyway, the bits and bobs got donated. Evy's grandmother never did get over the loss and passed on that same bitter regret to each generation of women. Now I see it's up for auction because jewelry has gone out again. Evy is going to be at my sleeve all night to buy it." A waiter wandered past with more champagne. Mr. Wilber nodded goodbye to Aerin and followed, his cane tapping the floor as he went.

Aerin had always liked Mr. Wilber. And she liked him even more now that he was likely to pay any price for a piece of jewelry from the auction catalogue.

She followed Mr. Wilber as he meandered through the crowd and found herself looking through the auction catalogue. She looked over his shoulder at the pictures of the family pendant. The huge, bright ruby surrounded by emerald cut rubies and baguette emeralds, set in filigreed gold took her breath away. Perhaps it was Royal Romanov, but the name in the catalogue was Mikhaylichenko-Romanov.

Russian royal lineage had always confounded Aerin, so she turned the page to the other items for auction. One that caught her eye was a sweet little Belle Époque platinum broach, large sapphires set with small diamonds in a bow shape. It would look great on her charcoal wool winter jacket. Overall it was prettier than it was valuable. The maker was a local man from the turn of the century, talented but not genius. She would definitely have to make sure Brett saw this piece. He loved her and he didn't mind when she bought attractive pieces of art.

She wandered off towards the band to admire the way they seemed to dance with their trumpets while they played. Big band music was an odd style to compliment a Degas theme, but it was undeniably festive. Her eyes drifted over to Mitzy again. Mitzy had lost a little of her aloof perfection in a fit of giggles with her assistant.

Mitzy took a cool drink of water to compose herself. The champagne had made her lightheaded already. Just a bit. She felt young and silly, but now was neither the time nor the place. Now was the time to make an impression.

She saw her parents enter at the side door. The arts gala was an event her mother looked forward to every year. Her father liked it because it was a swanky night on the town and put him good for the rest of the year. Her mother looked pretty and not a bit out of place. In fact, compared to the average age in the room, she was still young and vibrant. Her parents gravitated to a couple on the left of the room, obviously people they had met before.

"Pardon me, Sabrina. My parents are here and I think they can introduce me to some new friends."

"I'll be fine. Surely the stag nephew will join us sooner or later. I'd hate to miss that." Sabrina grinned.

"Oh, Mitzy, you look stunning!" Susan Neuhaus held her at arm's length and then pulled her in for a warm hug. She draped Mitzy's arm through her own and introduced her to her friends.

"Melanie, Rodger, this is my beautiful and successful daughter, Mitzy."

"Pleased to meet you," Mitzy said with a genuine smile.

"And you as well. Are we really meeting the famous Mitzy Neuhaus of radio, print and everywhere?" Rodger asked, with the deep throaty voice of an elderly smoker.

"From almost everywhere." Her eyes twinkled with delight as she accepted his compliments.

"Let me tell you, young woman, I heard what you said on the radio last week. That young man deserved a dressing down. I'm not entirely sure why you came back and apologized to him." He gave her a stern look.

"Oh, Rodger, you spend too much time listening to AM radio," his younger wife, Melanie chirped.

Foreclosed

"You know, Rodger, I had a hard time with it. I wondered what apologizing would do to my reputation as a hard hitting professional. But in the end, I didn't treat him with brotherly love at the time, did I? He has a problem, but I ought to have redirected his conversation politely and then spoken with him off of the air. In the end I knew I had to apologize to him in the same way that I had injured him, in public, on the air. It was the Christ-like thing to do."

"I thought it was lovely, Mitzy. I really did. I put my foot in my mouth all the time, but I never have the courage to apologize like you did." Melanie's face was full of genuine admiration.

Mitzy couldn't help but wonder if Melanie wanted her dear old husband to buy her a Victorian mansion.

"Have you looked through the auction catalogue yet?" Mitzy asked Melanie.

"I have. Isn't the Romanov piece something else? Can you imagine wearing that?" Melanie asked.

"No!" Mitzy laughed. "I'd be afraid to own such an important piece of jewelry. To borrow a phrase, 'it belongs in a museum.' But I really like the Belle Époque piece, platinum with sapphires."

"That was really pretty. It would look perfect with your hair and eyes," Melanie said.

"Thanks. I have my eye on it tonight. We'll see how bidding goes," Mitzy said.

"Dare I ask how business has been? With everything you hear in the papers, I was surprised a realty firm was able to host this evening's function."

"Oh, we would love more business, like everyone else, but we will survive this crisis."

"Come along, ladies," Roger said abruptly. "Let's get over to that bar for a real drink."

The crowd of gentlemen previously at the bar had moved on. Brett saw his parents and sister heading in his direction and stayed put. He thought he would do the nice and make some introductions for Mitzy. He knew how she thought, and knew she was only here to meet people who could still afford to buy property.

Aerin had brought the Wilbers to Brett where they were all chatting as Mitzy's crowd joined them.

"Mr. Wilber, Mrs. Simonite-Wilber. You remember my parents, Susan and Frank. But I don't think you've met my sister, Mitzy."

Mitzy smiled and shook Mr. Wilber's hand. "I'm very pleased to meet you both. I'm delighted by the evening so far, aren't you?"

"I don't know how truthfully Mr. Wilber can answer that for you. It looks to be a rather expensive evening for him." Mrs. Simonite-Wilber had a mischievous twinkle in her eye.

"Indeed?" Mitzy asked.

"Yes, indeed. My little wife here wants me to buy her a royal treasure." Mr. Wilber squeezed his wife's arm gently as he spoke.

Foreclosed

"He means to say that I want him to ransom my family heirlooms. And if he doesn't want to do it I will just have to use my own little auction paddle." She patted her handbag with a thin, shaky hand.

"Your family heirlooms are in the auction catalogue?" Mitzy asked.

"Indeed they are. My Grandmother's family jewels—Romanov you know. It turns out, they aren't good enough for the museum anymore so I thought my darling Mr. Wilber ought to purchase them back for me."

"And your daughter wants me to buy her a new boat. Do you want to tell her you got a necklace instead?" Mr. Wilber crossed his arms on his chest with a harrumph, but didn't seem as opposed to the idea as he was trying to sound.

"If our daughter loves the river, I don't see how that is my fault. You were the one who took her out every summer." And without acknowledging their new acquaintances, Mr. and Mrs. Wilber took their disagreement back in the direction of the auction catalogue.

"I was rather partial to the little Belle Époque piece," Mitzy said with a smile.

"Of course you were," Aerin snapped.

Mitzy caught the tone and changed the subject again. "Will any of you brave the lindy hop with me later? Dad?"

Her dad laughed and said yes. And then in the nature of cocktail parties they drifted apart again.

Mitzy came back to her seat at the table and saw Sabrina deep in conversation. All she could see were the broad shoulders and thick black hair of her dinner companion, possibly Adele's nephew. She got a perfectly clear view when she sat down.

Alonzo. Of course.

"Good evening," she said coolly.

Sabrina rocked her champagne flute on the table. "Well, Mitzy, you'll never guess who the stag nephew is. Handsome devil isn't he?" She patted Alonzo on the arm.

He stiffened. "I noticed that you had a...presence here." He picked up the table tent and read the welcome from Neuhaus notice again.

Adele rejoined the table at that moment. "Oh good, Alonzo, you are meeting people. I thought you might know Mitzy and Sabrina, since you all are in the same industry."

Alonzo cleared his throat. "They've done a good job with your promotional materials." He set the tent back in the middle of the table. He had been impressed by the mellow, understated tone to her new logo.

"Thank you," Mitzy said. "We handled them in-house. You know, I've wanted to be a part of this event for years and just this year had the opportunity. That is to say, Aerin, my sister-in-law, has been inviting me for years, but I've let my parents take the tickets." She was rambling a little. The girls in the office were right about one thing, Alonzo was worth looking at. He had deep black eyes and thick stubble on his square chin. His worst feature—make that his best feature, which was the worst part— was that he dimpled very nicely when he got around to smiling. He had tried to make use of those dimples in regards to her office space more than once.

Foreclosed

The thought of how rude he had been to her about the office space got her riled up again. She sat up a little straighter, if possible. Her alabaster shoulders glittered in the candlelight, set off by the line of her strapless black dress. "How has your hunt for office space been going, Alonzo?" she asked.

Adele looked at her with surprise. She hadn't expected that they might know each other well. She looked at Mitzy more carefully and measured the tension in the air. *This might be a very good match indeed,* she thought. Mitzy Neuhaus could keep up with her temperamental, brilliant nephew and frankly, had enough good looks to get his attention. It was obvious she had his attention. So obvious in fact, that Adele wondered why they weren't already seeing each other.

"I think you know, Mitzy, that there are very few spaces just right for my needs right now. I would love to get to work on renovating an office space. It would give my men some work, give them a job. I hate having them on rolling lay offs." He took what was supposed to be a casual drink of his coffee, but his fist clenched the cup.

Mitzy's heart fluttered. It hadn't occurred to her that he might want her space for that kind of reason. She assumed that he was selfish and bossy and rude—which he was. But apparently, he also cared about his crew. She coughed lightly and sipped her water.

"How's the radio show?" Alonzo asked, a little grin playing at the corners of his mouth. "I hear you are on more often now."

Mitzy noticed how closely Adele was watching them and decided to attempt to kill Alonzo with kindness. Or at least with politeness.

"It's going well. I'm enjoying being on more often. I bet the station would love to have someone like you in to sub for me now and again—someone less bitter."

He laughed. "If you've got more work than you can handle just call me, I'm sure I can fit you in. I'll be done with my little Baltimore Street project soon and have plenty of time for you."

She choked on her water. "Your what?"

"My little Baltimore Street project. I think the bank is going to be very interested in talking to us about it."

"If you do anything that hurts the value of that family neighborhood—"

"You mean of your Baltimore Street rental?"

"It is right next door to the Victorian. Debbie doesn't want to live by a business." She took a deep cleansing yoga breath. This was neither the time nor the place.

"Ow!" Sabrina had been jostled by someone behind her. She turned to look. "Watch out. Will you?" She seemed to be speaking to no one, but a well dressed waiter or busser or someone was moving along behind them and must have knocked into her. "I don't know what he got me with, but it was quite a jolt! Sorry, guys." Sabrina wasn't a bit sorry for interrupting. Even tipsy, she could tell it was time to distract them from what could have become an ugly scene.

Foreclosed

The auction finally came, after all of the dancing and what was a good, but rich dinner. The friendly seven at the table—Mitzy, Sabrina, Adele, Howard, and Alonzo, and the Mitchells who were on the board of directors, had managed to enjoy themselves through the entertainment. It was a table for eight but Alonzo and Mitzy had enough presence to make the empty plate disappear.

Everyone had a small white paddle with a black number on it for the auction. Sabrina tucked hers under her chair and drank the coffee that Mitzy had secured for her.

For most of the auction, the head table was appreciative, but quiet. Their bidding wasn't particularly expected. But then the Belle Époque piece came up. Many women in the crowd were interested in it, so the bidding quickly went over one thousand. Brett let Aerin know early on that the piece wasn't worth it to him. Aerin sat out the bidding.

Mitzy almost had it at $3900 when a last minute bid came from the back. She fought for it up to $4300 but was beginning to feel foolish. The last bid was just $4350 dollars, so she upped it once more to $4400—well above the actual value of the piece. She smiled, satisfied, as her bid was about to be accepted.

"Six thousand dollars."

She flipped in her chair and glared at Alonzo. "Six thousand dollars? Are you crazy?"

"Too rich for you, Mitz?" He smiled, his eyes laughing at her.

"Too stupid for me," she hissed at him.

"Oh, Alonzo, what a lovely piece," said Adele looked fondly at her nephew. "Do you have someone special in mind for it?" She turned and smiled at Mitzy.

"You are a special lady, Aunt Adele, but I think this time my mother is the most special." The men at the table guffawed at him. "Well played, Miramontes. Don't let anyone pin you down before you are ready," Mr. Mitchell said, his white mustache twitching as he laughed.

Things were quiet at their table until the Romanov-Mikhaylichenko pendant came up. A deeper hush fell over the room and the pendant was put up for an opening bid of one thousand dollars. Someone from the back of the room raised it from that to $5000 in one bid.

Mrs. Wilber's bidding war brought the price up to $15,000 before she dropped out.

Mitzy looked at Alonzo with a gleam in her eye and bid $15,500. It wasn't just a drop in the bucket anymore, but she hadn't been priced out entirely.

It went back and forth, until Mitzy had the high bid at $17,000.

"Twenty thousand dollars." Aerin held up her paddle, her mouth a firm line. Her forehead glistened but her paddle didn't shake. Brett put his drink down and cleared his throat.

"I would like to retire someday." Brett took a long drink from his tumbler.

"Don't be dramatic." Aerin held her paddle firm.

Mitzy's face was flushed and her breath was shallow.

Sabrina stared with her huge eyes.

Foreclosed

Mitzy's paddle stayed on the table.

The pendant was sold to Aerin Flint-Neuhaus.

Alonzo appraised Mitzy carefully. He didn't want to, but he had to respect her restraint in that moment. *There's a woman that doesn't act on impulse.* He added it to her short list of positive traits. Before this evening the list had been very short. The black dress had upped her positive points considerably, but a well dressed woman with self-control was altogether more rare and impressive.

Mitzy went home without any of the jewelry she had admired but also without the buyer's remorse she would have had. Aerin should be so lucky.

Mitzy shivered. She had made it through the whole evening without killing Alonzo Miramontes. There should have been an award for that. At times she even laughed at his jokes. He could tell a good story. She wondered if he might take her idea of going on the radio seriously.

They could be a good team.

She stopped. That hadn't really popped into her head, had it?

No. She was thinking of what would be good for the radio station, that's all.

A stocky, rather nondescript man of medium height and sandy brown-ish hair swept the floor of the Tiffany Center after the gala event. He had watched Aerin Flint-Neuhaus with care as she made her auction purchase official. And during the evening he had noted that Mitzy Neuhaus owned a rental property on a certain road called Baltimore.

Foreclosed

Chapter Eight

Sunday morning Mitzy needed to be refreshed. She didn't need responsibility or obligations. The morning was cool and gray. Rain was misting.

Her hair would need extra fortification today. She appraised herself in the mirror. Freshly washed, it looked almost the same as it had at the gala on Friday night. Loose, long and soft.

She put the can of hair spray down. *Forget it*, she thought. *Today is for me and God. Not clients or men.*

She left the house in more casual clothes, just jeans and a sweater. Perfect for light spring rain and anonymity. She drove right past her small family church. It would be a good day to disappear into a mega church, spend a Sunday without anyone asking her to join a project committee. She liked committees, but some days she just needed a Sabbath.

She went all the way across town, to the Westside, where she didn't buy any print ads. The big church on this side of town was New Life Ministries, some kind of non-denomination place famous for its good teaching and young pastor. Inside, she sunk into a green pew chair and opened her Bible. A few people greeted her in a friendly way, and she responded, but generally, they let her sit quietly and read.

By the end of the service she was ready to take communion. She had shed the frustration of the gala, of painful associations with people she didn't like and of the bad economy. She knew the peace might not last, but as she walked forward to take her bread and juice she only felt thankful.

She was thankful that her sister-in-law had allowed her to help with such a big part of her life, despite their differences.

She was thankful for having spent a fun evening with her friend Sabrina.

She was thankful that in this time of hardship for so many people she was able to be a blessing. She felt very blessed indeed to be able to be a blessing.

Her turn came at the little table in the front of the sanctuary. There were about ten white tablecloth covered tables at the front and at each one a lengthy line of people waited.

The waiting had been significant for her. She served herself the body and the blood, closed her eyes and thanked the Lord.

As she walked away from the table her eyes wandered down the line of tables. So many people partaking in the Lord's Supper together, each one of them giving themselves once more to God and His will.

It lifted her heart that so many people wanted God. If she could keep a tight hold on today's feeling she could do anything.

The man at the table next to her was kneeling, but she recognized him anyway. Who would have thought?

She was back to her seat by the time Alonzo had risen from his kneeling stance.

In her car, leaving the parking lot, Mitzy saw Alonzo helping a very old woman into his pickup truck. She wondered absently if it was his grandmother or someone else. At any rate, it was a surprising bit of nice to add to the overall picture.

She thought about what compromising her stance on her building would really mean.

How bad would it be to sell him half of her building?

If he had that project to do he might give up on his plans for the Victorian. And maybe he wasn't as awful as he seemed.

Monday morning, Joan stumbled through the front door of the office, her arms protecting a stylish, if somewhat large purse.

"Where's Mitzy?" Joan asked, puffing for breath.

"Getting coffee. Didn't you see her in the parking lot?" Sabrina eyed the bag. It was cute. Sort of high style. Not quite as artsy as she'd expect from Joan.

"She wasn't at Bean Me Ups. Maybe she went to make a donut run." Joan leaned against the wall.

"Sit down, make yourself comfortable." Sabrina waved her hand towards the empty chair at Mitzy's desk. "You know we're not doing anything very important right now." Out of the corner of her eye, Sabrina could have sworn that Joan's purse moved. She eyed it very closely. It had vented sides. "Joan...do you have a happy announcement to make?" Sabrina asked.

Joan sat down, sort of cradling her bag. "You're quick, come peek."

Sabrina peeked into a dog carrier masquerading as a bag. Inside was a small golden fluffy something. Very sweet.

"Ooh! Can I hold it?" Sabrina crooned.

"Of course." Joan lifted a fluffy, floppy eared puppy dog out of the purse and gently handed it over to Sabrina.

"What is it?" Sabrina asked, holding its soft fur to her cheek.

"He's a cock-a-poo."

"What?"

"A cocker spaniel poodle. He's the sweetest thing ever. A client of mine bought him last week while her husband was away on vacation. But when hubby came back he said no way, period, end of sentence." Joan set the dog carrier on Sabrina's desk. "She didn't dare tell him what the dog cost. I'm keeping track of him for a little bit, but I can't do it all day. I've actually got a new job starting. It's charming the way people turn to stagers after their house has sat for months on end instead of before." Joan pulled out Mitzy's chair and sat down. She stretched her arms and sighed deeply. "Do you know where I can find a good dog boarder?"

"A boarder? No, poor thing. Leave him here. We're not doing anything today. Do you have any puppy food for him?" Sabrina held the puppy up to her cheek and nuzzled him.

"Oh no, he ate. I can come back and get him before he needs anything else. I'll take a lunch and come see how you are doing. Listen, if it is really okay, I'll leave him. I've got to run now." Joan stood up again. "Promise me it's not a problem, or he won't stay." Joan stepped towards the door, ready to make her break.

"Wittle himsy a problem? Never!" Sabrina held him over her head and wiggled him like a baby.

Joan had the door open before Sabrina finished her sentence. "My client called him Gilbert. Have fun, you two."

Joan had been gone for quite a while before Mitzy returned with her coffee and donuts. But not long before Ben showed up with his sarcasm and complete disbelief over what idiots women can be at times.

Mitzy brought in coffee and donuts. Not from Bean Me Ups, which doesn't sell donuts, but from Winchells, a Portland classic. She set them on the reception counter and sniffed the air. "Do you smell that?"

Sabrina blushed.

"Is it a sort of Lysol meets dog pee kind of smell?" Ben laughed.

"Well, yes. It is."

"Then yes, I smell it too."

"So…is it too obvious to ask why we smell that?" Mitzy was looking the not gigantic room over as she asked.

"It's Gilbert's fault." Ben jerked his thumb in Sabrina's direction.

"Gilbert?" Mitzy turned her attention to Sabrina. The can of Lysol air spray was on her desk. A magenta bag with vented sides was on the floor, in the knee hole of the desk, but Mitzy saw it.

"He's just a puppy, Ben. What do you expect?" Sabrina nudged the carrier with the toe of her Birks, pushing it farther under the desk.

"Puppy?" Mitzy was catching on slowly.

"He's awful sweet, Mitz. He's a cock-a-poo, and velvety soft, so fluffy and tiny. Really tiny, come see." Sabrina lifted a small, slightly damp puppy out of the bag from the floor.

"Sabrina! He's all wet. Didn't you take him out?" Mitzy turned her head and looked sideways at the messy, sort of smelly little dog.

"Should I take him out? I thought that's what the bag was for."

"You didn't!" Mitzy groaned.

"Umm. I kind of did. It says washable." Sabrina turned tomato red.

"Then go wash it, and the puppy. Run to the bathroom, use warm water and no soap. Or wait, I have some baby shampoo in my desk. Use that." Mitzy dug in her desk drawer and pulled out a sample sized bottle of shampoo. She couldn't let the dog derail her plans, so she worked hard to maintain a sense of equanimity.

"So, can I ask why you keep a bottle of baby shampoo in your desk?" Ben crossed his arms and leaned back in his chair, an amused smile playing on his face.

"It's not as mysterious as why Sabrina is keeping a puppy under her desk. I keep a change of clothes in the closet. If I get a stain I can hand wash it right away. I'm certainly not going to use bathroom hand soap on anything silk. But really, why the puppy?" Sounds of crying puppy and splashing water were coming from the ladies' room.

"Sounds like Sabrina could use your change of clothes too," was all Ben offered.

"If she's learned anything working here, she has her own. Why a puppy?" The last bit she projected so Sabrina could hear her.

From the bathroom came, "Joan!"

"Joan." Mitzy picked out a maple bar. This was not a good day for a stinky office. Curt was going to call again about the film crew, and most likely want to see her office. If she could, she'd have them film the signing in her small, private office. It was charming, had good light. Simple, quality craftsman furniture picked up bit by bit at the antiques mall down the road. He'd want to see the office though and today it smelled bad. They would be much more likely to film at Xavian's Bistro two blocks down if he thought her office was a dump. Well, not a dump, but a place that smelled too bad to spend the day in for filming.

All she wanted to do right now was sell a house. She'd gladly trade her donut and the TV show for a nice, hopeful couple in the back of the company HHR driving around looking for their dream house. That was really the only way she wanted to spend the day.

Sabrina popped out of the bathroom with the wet puppy wrapped in her Lands End cardigan. He was much cuter wet and clean than he had been filthy.

"I have the carrier drying in the sink." She tried to pass the puppy to Ben. He refused impolitely.

"Oh, give him to me." Mitzy reached for Gilbert.

"I'll just run back in the bathroom for a second and dry the carrier with some paper towels."

She came back in a moment with the dry, clean carrier.

The warm wiggling dog made Mitzy's pulse slow down. She held him close to her heart. "Sabrina, if you are going to keep him here all day, you have to take him outside to the planter box to potty every twenty minutes. You can't let him go in his carrier. For one thing it makes him miserable. For another…well, it still stinks in here."

Sabrina looked down at her feet.

"What is it?"

"I took him out to play for a few minutes," Sabrina said quietly.

"And?" Mitzy raised her eyebrow.

"He had an accident on the rug." Sabrina glanced towards a dark stain near Ben's chair.

"And you tried to clean it with air deodorizer?" Mitzy pressed the dog closer to her chest and let out a slow breath. She could keep calm, if she tried.

"It said disinfecting…" Sabrina chewed her bottom lip and looked up at Mitzy.

"It smells horrible." A warm spot began to develop on Mitzy's blouse. Mitzy scratched Gilbert behind his ear and then placed him in his carrier gently.

Ben snorted.

Sabrina offered a little smile.

Mitzy exhaled slowly, through her mouth. "Sabrina, take the puppy and your sweater home. Then go to the pet shop. Buy disposable puppy pads and enzyme floor spray. I'm going to change my blouse, put it to soak, and that would be why I have the baby shampoo, Ben. Then I am going to beg the carpet cleaners to get here immediately." Mitzy took her change of clothes out of the closet.

Her phone rang.

Sabrina flew out of the office as quick as she could. She did not seem to notice that she had left the puppy under her desk.

Mitzy took her cell phone into the bathroom with her to change.

"Mitzy, baby!" the caller said.

"Yes, Curt?" Mitzy pulled one sleeve off.

"We made it to town and I want to see you today." Curt sounded like he was eating something.

"That will be wonderful. I was hoping it would work out." She slipped the other arm out of the other sleeve.

"We are going to see three other applicants today—but they are the buyers. The market is crazy right now and we wanted to secure four episodes while we are here. No point in coming this far out and not getting something done." In fact, it sounded like Curt was eating and in a car. Or more hopefully eating somewhere outside where there was traffic.

"I think that sounds like a wise idea. This is the best time of year to be filming in Portland." Mitzy got three buttons undone, which was harder with a tiny cell phone pinned between her shoulder and her ear than she had thought it would be. She was wishing she had done the buttons first, and then the sleeves.

"Can your client meet up with us today as well?" Curt asked.

What with the gala and her Victorian obsession, Mitzy hadn't taken the time to line up her client. And they had no buyers waiting. "Curt…" She was determined to be completely truthful, even if she felt like a fool. "I don't have anyone lined up. My stager has a client and I was hoping to talk to them about the show, but I don't have any buyers right now."

"That's okay, babe." He had called her baby and babe more working together for House Hunters than he had in the two years they dated. "We've got our people and we'll find a match for you. You work on your client. We'll try and get you in two episodes, okay? We'll talk about the wrap up shoot when we sign papers." There was honking, rather loud honking.

It would be like Curt, Mitzy thought, to be eating, talking on the phone and driving a rented convertible at the same time. "When would you like to meet?" she asked, slipping her shirt off and catching it with her free hand.

"Let's do this after lunch."

"Can we go even later?" she asked as she unfolded her v-neck sweater.

"You have something in mind?" Curt said around a mouthful of food.

"Let's meet here at the office at five." She held the phone away from her head for a moment, while she quickly pulled the sweater over her head.

She caught back up with Curt mid-sentence. "Then afterwards we can come right over. Five sounds fine. Want to do dinner when we are done with business?"

"I'd love to. We'll see you at five, Curt."

"Five it is." Curt hung up and Mitzy followed.

Curt and the House Hunters team were coming at five.

Mitzy got Chem-Dry on the phone. She begged and pleaded and now they were coming at noon to clean the floors, promising to be done by two at the latest.

So House Hunters was coming. But in the meantime she had work to do.

It took a few telephone transfers to get to the person who knew anything about it, but apparently there was a decent offer on the Victorian on Baltimore Street. No, she couldn't know what the offer was. Yes, the owner of the home wanted to accept it and the bank was deciding if they would approve a short sale.

Mitzy made a call. "Alonzo Miramontes, you are already buying that Victorian. You made it sound like I still had a chance. You lied to me."

Her voice was icy. Whatever she had thought about him at church the day before was a distant memory.

"I said I was going to talk to the bank. I didn't need to run it by you for approval. It's not your listing." He said with a growl.

"This weekend at the gala, you sat and chewed the fat with me for four hours and made like you hadn't started the process of buying the house. But in reality the bank is already processing the short sale."

"What makes you think they are working on my offer?" His voice relaxed, more false innocence and less angry growl.

"It is you. Who else wants that old dump besides me and you? I want to know—did you offer enough that the lien holders will get their money? Did you?" Mitzy was storming up and down the office. Ben had himself tucked into his desk as close as he could get.

"That is for the bank to decide, isn't it?" He was brisk and almost professional now.

"I have friends who have—oh never mind. I thought you understood these things. At the gala when you talked about work for your crew, I thought you were a decent guy."

"Neuhaus, I am a decent guy. And if I want to buy an inn for my sister to run and to give my guys a job to work then I am going to buy it. I don't really care if you approve." He paused.

Mitzy wondered if he was distracted by something or drinking coffee. Then she wondered if he took cream in his coffee.

"I've got work to do. I hope you find something to occupy yourself with." Alonzo hung up.

Mitzy squeezed in a response that indicated she was done, so he hadn't actually hung up on her, but it was close.

She was fuming. Steaming. The puppy made some whining noises, so she grabbed him up and hustled into the cold spring morning. She put him into the planter box. "Do your business, will you?"

Sabrina beat the carpet cleaners back to the office. She had the spray, the puppy pads, an assortment of chic dog accessories, and a crate.

They crated Gilbert and gave him some very soft treats. They took him to the box every twenty minutes. Even Ben had to admit that it was nice to see the girls with something to do.

After a long day of trying to reconnect with Joan, Mitzy gave up. Joan was clearly in her groove shopping, arranging and creating atmosphere. After the meeting with the House Hunters execs, which was rather uneventful, Mitzy declined dinner with Curt.

"Don't say that. You need to eat, I need to eat. I won't even make you go to the Olive Garden." Curt gave her a winning grin. That had been his favorite restaurant while they were together.

"I've got this puppy see…" she said, as she cuddled the soft pup.

"Where can we eat with the puppy? This is Portland, I'm sure we could go almost anywhere."

"If you won't take it as a come on, I'd just as well take you back to the condo and eat some Chinese."

"That sounds great. And I won't take it as a come on. If anyone knows you are not that kind of girl, I know it." He picked through Sabrina's collection of doggy goodies and pulled out a strange sack like contraption. Sabrina had left them all behind when she went home. There was a strict no pets policy at her apartment. "Use this. You'll love it." He tossed her a thing that seemed to be a baby sling for puppies.

"Lovely." Mitzy was surprised at how easy it was to put on. She nestled the puppy into the pocket of the sling and found that really, she did love it. It would only be better if the puppy could purr.

They sat on her patio, eating Chinese from Safeway off of plastic plates with chopsticks. It was chilly still, in early spring, so she had her little patio heater on, making a warm orange glow. They watched as dusk rolled in and the families around the condo community called their kids in and turned on their patio lights.

"So you are in show business now too?" Curt asked.

"Sort of. I've got a radio segment that seems to have gotten away from me." Mitzy was feeling a bit annoyed by the way the radio station seemed to think she wanted to give them free entertainment. They acted like she should be grateful for the advertising. Once her Wednesday morning segment had morphed into a daily morning chat fest with Johnny who had gotten only slightly less obnoxious, she felt like the balance had altered and she was now providing for them. It was something she planned to renegotiate in the next day or two.

"Gotten away from you, like you lost it, or like it exploded in popularity?"

"I wouldn't say exploded in popularity. But I had a...scene...with the co-host that had listeners listening and so they sort of upped me from my weekly spot to a daily. I think I am using it well, but they think they are giving me free advertising. You know?"

"The relationship between the advertisers and the entertainers has always been tricky. Do you get lots of free stuff from the station?"

She laughed, and nearly spilled her coke. "As a matter of fact I do. I have seen every show in town this season, which has been fun. But there have been times I would have sworn the only people at the theater were comp tickets." Mitzy set her soda on the side table. She rubbed her cold hands together. "It's a hard time right now. I don't see the way out of it. I mean, I see a number of roads out, but they are all hard and leave a lot of people hurting for a long time. Back to free stuff, that heater was a comp. Pretty great, no? I don't know how the radio got their hands on patio furniture, but it was delivered to the office with a note with love from the Station. It's been very handy."

"And footy," Curt said, stretching his long legs out to the warm glow. "I could get used to lying around. I bet this is what you do all day long, lounging around resting on your laurels, plenty comfy until someone is ready to buy a house." Curt grinned.

"Yeah, right. That's so me, isn't it? I've got employees to feed. I can't just sit around. I can pay them, but they have this funny thing called pride and don't want to sit around the office doing nothing all day. I can appreciate it, but making work for them is getting to be a lot of work for me." She chuckled softly and Curt joined her. She had the sick feeling that their hard times were just beginning.

"I bet you do, too. I bet you make up things to keep them busy all day so they can feel like they've earned it."

"We're a team. The success we've had that makes the business able to pay their checks is due in large part to their hard work. Why do you think I applied to be on TV?"

"Because you are star struck? Fame obsessed? Desperate to reconnect with old flames?"

"Because it gave my assistant something to do for the afternoon. I've got an idea for a local TV show. On the one hand developing the proposal gives my assistant something to do. On the other hand once it is accepted it gives most of the staff more weekly tasks to get done and educates the public—to help them get through the crisis. We've got to revitalize real estate if we ever want to get out of this recession."

"You should have your own show. A real one, on HGTV. You'd be fantastic."

"But of course." She laughed again, but it felt hollow. He used to tell her that all the time, back when they had been in love. But she knew she was too tall, gangly, and goofy looking to be on TV. "Not my own show, just a segment on the local morning show. The show that people watch while they get ready for work, or after they take their kids to school. Pardon me, but people watch HGTV to lose themselves in a fantasy or to figure out a way to fix a house problem. People watch morning shows to keep up on what's going on in the neighborhood."

"You've got this business all figured out, don't you? You always have." He smiled ruefully. He'd fallen in love a few times since Mitzy but it was never with someone he wanted to marry.

"I love the business. I have to know it."

They cleaned up their plates in relative quiet. He talked about life on the road with the show. She talked about the Victorian.

"It sounds like you really love the house," he said, leaning on the wall by the door.

"I don't know. I think I love what it represents. Or what it could represent. If I could get the authorities to take this kind of crime seriously, and if I could get the right person to buy the house…I just want everything to get better." Mitzy sighed. Such dreams. What could one house really fix? What could one Realtor really fix? She knew the answer, but she hated it. "I guess the house is kind of symbolic to me. If I can make this one thing right, and all of us try to make one thing right, we can get out of this. I know I didn't cause the house bubble to burst, but Realtors, mortgage brokers, people without a clue to reality did, and I am a part of them." She looked past Curt, into what she wished and hoped for, but was beginning to doubt.

She was lost for the night. She needed to get down on her knees and pray, and she knew it. Whenever she thought she was capable of saving the world, it was time to get down on her knees and talk to the One who really was.

"I'll try and get the house on TV, Mitz. Maybe that will help." They shook hands in a friendly way and he left.

Foreclosed

Chapter Nine

The next day dawned a bright, crisp spring morning and Mitzy was feeling optimistic. A night of prayer had a way of doing that. Nothing material had changed, but inside she remembered, at least for now, that the fate of the world wasn't in her hands.

A few things on her agenda were looking up too. She was getting calls in the office—mostly fans of her extended radio spot, but also people with genuine real estate questions.

Some of them insisted on talking to her, but others were willing to take advice from her staff. A ringing phone gave everyone pep.

Ben had even gotten a few design jobs from people who liked her stuff at the gala.

Foreclosed

She did a few deep breathing stretches and limbered up for what looked to be a fun, exciting day.

She had to pop into the radio station early this morning. Ostensibly, she provided twenty minutes of morning chatter with Johnny, but it often went longer and no one complained. So long as traffic and weather got their time and no commercials were shorted, she was considered a welcome guest.

Listeners seemed to like it when she put Johnny in his place, which she tried to do as little as possible.

She liked it when she could give peppy encouraging talk to families about money, real estate and keeping on in the down turn.

She always forwarded her office calls to her cell when the office was closed. It wasn't unusual to have at least one call on the way into the station.

When her phone rang, she was flying down the highway in her Miata with the top down. She had her blue tooth head set on so she took the call. "Mitzy Neuhaus, good morning."

The good morning came screeching to a halt.

She raced to her rental unit on Baltimore. She had just enough time to drive by and see the extent of the damage before she hit the radio station. She pulled into the driveway and gawked at what was before her.

The walls on the front and one side were charred and she could see in through spots. The fire fighters had put it out before it hit the roof or took down a wall in its entirety.

The fire had started the night before, while Debbie was out having dinner so she was safe, but her cat was missing.

She was a wreck when she called Mitzy. She had no idea how it had started. She felt terrible, was scared and embarrassed. She didn't smoke or light candles, hadn't been ironing or making coffee. She just had no idea. There was an inquiry and until then she was moving in with her sister.

Mitzy spoke to her in calm, low tones and said obviously, with no house to live in she wasn't expected to pay the rent. She offered several platitudes about how glad she was that Debbie was safe.

But was Debbie safe?

Was it just faulty wiring, or was someone trying to hurt her?

Mitzy was hoping it was a wiring issue. Debbie worked for the Red Cross and was highly regarded as a good, kind woman. Who would want to burn her house down?

Mitzy wasn't permitted in the house yet and didn't have time anyway, so she drove from Baltimore Street to the radio station, ready for war.

She didn't know who she'd be in war with, but pretty much everyone had better toe the line. She wasn't ready to kick the puppy or anything that drastic. But his soft, warm, fuzziness in the sling across her chest was incongruous to her mood, so she dumped him in the dog carrier.

She would definitely be talking about stupid people who purchase and then immediately abandon pets during her time on the radio this morning. Who does that kind of thing?

Foreclosed

The image of her burned out rental was seared in her mind's eye. What kind of person burned up someone's home?

It crossed her mind that someone who wanted her off of his tail about a certain house next door, might do this kind of thing.

The day didn't get better from there. Her time on the radio dragged and she felt like a big complainer.

Johnny made a comment to the effect of 'Mitzy the grouch' and her cousin Oscar. But her worst moment was when she said, "It's just too stupid for words, Johnny. People are just too stupid for words." That was not an endearing or uplifting sentiment to be sharing on the radio.

The calls that came in to the office indicated she was right—people were stupid, but they hated to have it pointed out. Worse, the puppy piddled on the carpet in the radio booth. It stunk. She left the mess for the radio janitorial staff (if there was such a thing) to take care of.

Sabrina was annoyed at having to take grouchy radio listener calls and Joan still couldn't be found to collect the puppy.

Everyone was on pins and needles waiting to hear back from Curt.

Mitzy wanted to go back in time to before the trip to her rental and start the day over.

But she couldn't and things just didn't get better. The police stopped by a little after lunch.

"Mitzy Neuhaus?" a tall, tan officer asked, flipping open his badge.

"No, I'm sorry, I'm her assistant Sabrina," Sabrina said politely.

"I'm Mitzy Neuhaus." Mitzy turned from her desk, which was against the wall.

"We'd like to talk to you about the auction you attended last weekend. Would you like to talk here or come down to the station?"

The officer was young and being very polite, so she couldn't possibly be in trouble, she hoped.

"We can speak privately in the office here. Sabrina was also at the auction, should she join us?"

"We'll talk to you both separately," the officer said.

Mitzy led the officers into the small private office and took a chair. They both remained standing.

"At the auction you bid on some jewelry items. Can you describe them for us?"

"One of them was…I think it was platinum with diamonds and sapphires. I mean, it had larger sapphires and small, accent diamonds. It was locally made about a hundred years ago. It was very pretty, a sort of bow shape." She didn't ask any questions, but waited with nervous tension while they took their notes.

"Did you win this auction item?"

"No."

"Can you recall who won it?" they asked, eyeing her closely.

"Alonzo Miramontes."

"Do you know Mr. Alonzo Miramontes?"

"Yes."

"How well do you know him, Ms. Neuhaus?"

"We are acquainted through business."

"And how did you feel about his winning the item?" Their posture was stiff, polite yet unyielding. She had no idea why they were questioning her and was beginning to feel nervous.

"I felt like…like he paid too much. But that it was sweet because he said he was giving it to his mother."

"You heard him say this?"

"Yes." Mitzy tapped the toe of her boot against the leg of the table.

"And how did you hear him say this?"

"We were seated at the same table."

"And the other pieces you bid on?" His voice maintained an even tone that Mitzy was beginning to find very intimidating.

"Just one—the Romanov pendant."

"Did you win this item?"

"No, I did not."

"Do you know who won the item?"

"Yes, my sister-in-law did." Mitzy drummed her fingers in time to her tapping toe. It felt like the officer had a wire tap to all of her little jealousies.

"And what did you think about that?"

"I thought that she had won a beautiful piece of jewelry and made a generous donation." Mitzy stood and pressed the palms of her hands together to make them stop shaking. "What is this about?"

"The night of the auction the museum was robbed and the jewelry that had been sold at auction was stolen. We are talking to everyone who bid on the pieces." They shut their little notebooks and led Mitzy out the door of her small office. Then they ushered Sabrina in.

Before they left, they stopped at the reception desk. "We're talking to everyone who bid at the auction and really appreciate your cooperation. We will call you if we need to speak to you further."

Mitzy spoke carefully, hoping her voice wouldn't shake. "We will be allowed to have our lawyers present next time?" The line of questions did not make her comfortable or happy. And Sabrina had looked downright scared when she exited the little room.

The officer leaned on the reception desk. "Ms. Neuhaus, you really aren't a suspect, I swear. We do have someone in mind but have to sort of 'eliminate' everyone else. The event was a real 'Who's Who' in Portland kind of night, so we want to cross all of our Ts and dot our Is especially since your brother is involved. We want everything above board."

It was small comfort. She didn't let her guard down, but spoke in a kind voice. "Then the four of us can chat—you all and my brother and I—next time you have any questions."

The officers got the hint, tipped their hats and left.

Sabrina looked at Mitzy.

Mitzy looked at Sabrina.

Sabrina nodded almost imperceptibly. She grabbed her laptop bag.

"Don't forget that smart phone thing," Mitzy said.

As the door swung shut behind them Ben looked up. "Hey, where are you guys…oh never mind." He turned his head back to his computer.

Foreclosed

The Miata squealed into the parking lot of the museum. It was quiet outside, but the lines of school buses indicated inside the museum was a different story.

"Perfect," Mitzy said. "I'm going to distract Aerin. If I know her she is cranky and upset and will talk and talk. The staff is overrun with children who want to pick at the paintings so no one will notice you. Sneak off to use the ladies' room, but really visit the office. In fact, we will both be in the office chatting up Aerin and you just slip off to use the private bath. But try and get near the janitorial office, or whatever it is. Maybe security."

"Really? Can't I be the one to talk to Aerin?" Sabrina gave a pathetic doe eyes look to her friend.

"Sure, why not?" Mitzy grinned.

"Well…okay, maybe I don't want to."

Mitzy knew that Sabrina had been grilled by Aerin before about art and had no wish to repeat the experience. Especially while Aerin was upset.

"When you find the security room, talk to the guys at the desk, if there are any. Probably there will be since the kids are there. Ask about security tapes from the break-in. If they will show them to you, try and get some pictures. I want to know who busted into the museum."

"Do you really think the security guys will show me their tapes?" Sabrina asked.

Mitzy chewed on her cheek. She wanted them to show Sabrina the tapes, but that wasn't quite the same. "No. So maybe spill your coffee on the keyboard and cause a ruckus. You'll figure it out."

Mitzy brought a tray of coffee with her to the admin offices.

"Is Aerin in?" Mitzy handed a coffee to the receptionist.

The receptionist put the coffee on her desk like it was dirty

"Let me see." She wrinkled her nose at Mitzy. "May I ask who is here to see her?"

"Mitzy." She smiled her biggest smile and scanned the room for security devices.

The receptionist picked up the phone and spoke in almost inaudible tones.

"She's just leaving the building, but she'll be back shortly. You can wait in her office."

Aerin must have slipped away as soon as she hung up the phone. Her office was completely deserted when Mitzy and Sabrina entered it.

Mitzy went straight to the file cabinet and started rifling through.

"Mitzy!" Sabrina gaped at Mitzy. "What are you doing?"

"I'm looking for the gala files. I'm sure she has a ton of them in paper. I want to know who stole the jewelry."

"I know you want to know who stole the jewelry, but this can't be legal."

"Sure it's not. Here." She pulled out a fat blue file folder and laid it gently on the desk. She opened it and began to turn pages. Sabrina leaned over her shoulder for a better look.

"Buckingham Tea pulled out as their sponsor," Mitzy read.

"Really? They are huge. I wonder why they pulled out?"

"Me too." On the other hand, Buckingham Tea was too big to steal a few pieces of jewelry. She needed to find an individual, not a corporation.

"Do you think it's important?" Sabrina's voice was hushed and anxious.

"No."

"Oh."

They kept turning pages.

"Here's a whole stack of auction notes. Pages of history on the jewelry. Get out your phone."

Sabrina fumbled for her phone, but got it out.

"Hurry and take a picture of each page as I turn them."

There were about twenty pages and they got them all on the phone. "I hope we can read those later," Mitzy said, eyeing the little phone suspiciously.

She closed the folder and put it back in the drawer. What else could she dig into while she waited for Aerin? Unlimited access to this office was a much better opportunity than sending Sabrina to the security office, if only she knew how to use it. She looked around the room, but couldn't tell what was important to her case.

Sabrina was helping herself to the computer. "Look! I can access the security cameras from Aerin's desktop! Cool. I wonder why she left it all logged on?"

"Probably because she didn't expect we were coming to spy." Mitzy leaned in over Sabrina's shoulder this time, her heart beating in her ears. This was a good thing, she hoped.

Sabrina navigated the system pretty well and got images from the night of the break-in up. Mitzy held the smart phone and snapped pictures.

The door to the office opened.

Mitzy stood up, smooth as butter. "Good morning," she said warmly.

It wasn't her sister at the door.

"Can I help you?" Mitzy asked. She stood, shoulders back, and a tight smile on her face. She wanted to look like she had every right to be there. And it seemed to her she did have as much right to be in her sister-in-law's office as this janitor did.

Sabrina had quietly returned the computer screen to the desktop and leaned back in her chair, smiling.

Mitzy held the phone against her hip but didn't hide it.

"This is Ms. Flint-Neuhaus' office," the man said with a soft voice. He had a thick blond mustache and a service station style hat, pulled low over his eyes.

"Yes. She asked us to wait for her here."

He cleared his throat and looked around, somewhat nervously. "I'll come back and clean later." He kept his eyes on the floor and slipped back out the door.

Mitzy had clicked a picture of him, but got him as his head was turning. It seemed odd to have a janitor pop in mid-morning to clean an office.

Sabrina and Mitzy were edgy now. They were anxious to get back to the privacy of the Miata so they could review their information. They waited five more minutes in silence.

"I don't think she's coming back," Sabrina said.

"Neither do I." Mitzy let out a breath she had been holding. Her stomach was twisted. Aerin would be horrified if she knew they had violated her privacy.

She left a mocha on Aerin's desk with a note of sympathy hastily scribbled on some Neuhaus New Homes notepaper from her purse and they left. She told herself that spying was a small wrong compared to the thief whose acts had put her in the eye of the police for something she hadn't done.

After reading the auction files, Mitzy knew more about the jewelry than most of the people who used to own it had known.

She had also studied and studied the screen shots of the robbery, but it was no use. A lot of blurry pictures of blurry film of a person of slight build in some kind of mask and hat—probably a ski mask—busting into the safe. They were still shots, so she didn't even know if he had broken the lock or picked it.

She processed what she knew and drew a few small conclusions. Her new ideas just left her with more questions.

The thief knew where to find the jewels. The thief knew his time to get the jewels away from the museum was limited. Did he know when the items were going to be transferred to their new owners? Did he know who those new owners were? Had he been present at the auction?

She spent that evening at her parents' house. She had been on her own for thirteen long years, but she still went home and put her head on her mom's shoulder when she needed comfort. She even left work early. It seemed like the world was just spinning out of her control.

They sat on the overstuffed sofa, a warm afghan thrown over them and had a mommy and daughter snuggle in front of the television.

"Do you think it was right for me to start in on this house thing?"

Susan turned her eyes from the TV. "Hmmm? What's that, honey? What do you mean, 'this house thing'?" She was reclining on the arm of the sofa, while Mitzy snuggled down with her. Susan's arm was thrown over her daughter casually and she rubbed her back, mothering her, while they watched the show.

"I got so mad when I saw someone had been stealing improvements from the Victorian. At the time it seemed like getting the house some attention, and getting it sold would be a good project. It would keep everyone busy and solve a little problem. But the problems have escalated far beyond an unpaid bill at the stoneworks."

Gilbert the puppy had Susan's lap. She scratched him behind his ears absently. "Things have gotten pretty hectic for you, honey, but I don't see how the puppy or the robbery are related to the old house. Or even each other. I think you worry too much."

"Maybe I do," she said softly. But she continued to worry about it.

When Mitzy got home that night she called her brother.

Brett Neuhaus was tall and lean like Mitzy. He had scant brown hair and a long face. He wore round spectacles and was rather bookish in appearance. His looks completely belied his reputation in the courtroom. He was a tiger on trial and had a record of wins longer than most attorneys with twice the years under their belt.

"Our home was burgled too. Same night as the museum but I'd say right before. Aerin and I went out for drinks after the event with the other development folks. We've got a sort of all-nighter kind of tradition. They are all always completely wiped out, but too excited to sleep." When we got home, we saw immediately that we had been robbed. They didn't get anything. They cracked the safe but left everything intact. It was very strange. Our alarm system was activated, but the burglar was gone before the cops arrived. We talked to them that night, around three when we got home. And then they called us the next day to talk about the museum. It's just ridiculous. That pendant isn't worth half of what Aerin paid for it. Who would go to all that trouble for one pendant? In fact, we know it was just for one pendant. The auction items hadn't been distributed yet and were found discarded not a mile from the museum. And of course, the only one missing was the pendant."

"That is really crazy. But maybe the piece is worth more than we think. Maybe there is a Russian market for it. I hear the government in Russia is trying to get back certain items that used to be in the royal treasury." Mitzy was still frazzled by her encounter with the police and found it very disturbing that her brother's home had been broken into.

"How do you know things like that, Mitzy?" Brett asked, doubting her sources as a good lawyer should.

"I saw it on the

Antiques Road Show. Someone had a Faberge egg and the expert talked for a long time about the value of keeping track of the history of your piece. A Faberge egg that the Russian government had its sights on might have to be forfeit. So maybe…maybe someone has their mind set on collecting Russian valuables, for the government, or for some kind of big sting or something."

"Seems possible. We have a pretty heavy Russian Mafia out here." Brett picked his fingernails while he talked.

"Really? That's so…"

"It's not racist, Mitzy. It just is. The Russian community doesn't like it either. I know the law is trying to knuckle down on them, but we just don't have any good connections."

"What about this house? Some Mikhaylichenko fellow sold it about a year ago. That was the same name as the pendant. I wonder if we could find him and sort of feel him out."

Foreclosed

"You were all up in arms about the current owner taking away his improvements. Maybe I should try and prosecute him. We'd get the house in the public eye. Who knows what we could drag up?"

"That sounds risky and not necessarily legal. At least that's what I keep hearing from the police. Mills has only sort of possibly committed a crime."

"Sort of possibly, until there is precedent. I'm going to talk to some people about it. I'd like the State to take Mills on. It's about time we stop living without law and order."

"I like the idea."

"Tell you what, sis, hint at it on the radio, okay? We want people to believe in this case. If it is a case. And it might not even have to become a case really. We just have to pursue it. Get the right people interested and it could really take off. What we need is to get the city council excited about it. They make things happen in this town."

Chapter Ten

The idea was an interesting one and Mitzy brought it up on the air immediately the next morning. The town knew right away that that hot shot lawyer Neuhaus was on the case and he wasn't one to let up.

"You've got your hound dog brother on this guy's trail now, huh?" Johnny snorted.

"I don't 'have' anyone on any trail. Brett Neuhaus is as sick as I am of living in the Wild West. This is a land of law and order and it is about time that people figured it out."

"Are you sure you aren't thinking of Salt Lake City?"

"Portland may be a bit…quirky…but it shouldn't be a dangerous place. And yet, in the time since I first got all riled up about the property theft situation, The Arts Council of Portland was robbed, my brother's home was broken into, there was what I think was an attempt at fraud perpetrated in regards to a home I have listed for sale. This is ridiculous. If this is the little circle of crime in just my arena, what is everyone else facing?"

"Maybe it's the company you keep, Mitzy," Johnny said.

"I am spending a good deal more time here with you," she rejoined.

"Ouch, sister. I ain't no trouble to no one." Johnny smiled.

"I'll let your conscience be the judge of that."

They opened the morning for calls and heard tale after tale of people getting cheated—kicked when they were down. A few people hoped that Brett would get his man.

But there were just as many people begging her to reconsider her stance, that when you were losing it all, it just made sense to try and get as much cash flow as you could. She found their desperation sad.

It was just sad all around.

Back at the office, Sabrina was hysterical and Ben was walking around like an insulted rooster.

"We called and called and called you," Sabrina sobbed.

"We thought you'd want to know right away." Ben stood in the doorway of the office, his arms crossed over his chest.

The three of them were standing outside of the office building while a couple of young police officers sorted through their livelihood which was strewn across the floor inside.

"I don't check my phone while I'm on the air. You knew where I was. Why didn't you call the station? They'd have gotten hold of me." The sight of the police had turned her melancholy to fear. She shivered though the morning was bright. She'd seen too much of the police lately.

"The glass was broken in the door, so I called the cops right away," Sabrina said. "I came in at ten today, it just seemed right, with not much going on."

Mitzy looked at her watch. It was only ten-thirty. Some of her guilt rolled off. She hadn't left these kids here too long alone. "It's okay. I'm here now. Have you been inside yet?"

"No, we were waiting for you. We knew you'd be here."

A young, short cop cleared his throat. "You all can come in now and tell us what is missing and make your police report."

Their particular office was quite small; the reception area, just a couple of square feet, the common office a nice size, twenty by twenty, two restrooms and the private office. Papers were scattered everywhere but, besides the door, nothing had been destroyed.

They detailed to the officers the amount of disarray they found everything in and duly reported the break-in. Then they had a pow-wow.

"Break-ins at the office are no good. I don't know how to keep us safer than everything I've already done." Mitzy turned her head, taking in the damage. "I don't understand why the computers are still here." Mitzy tried to piece together what a boss does after a break-in, but felt at a loss.

"You don't?" Ben said giving his aging Mac an indignant look.

Foreclosed

"Oh. Well. No, they aren't much value. Or they don't look like it at least. But they've got decent upgrades inside."

"Barely decent."

"We seem like the kind of place that you'd hit for identity theft. Let's sort out this huge paper mess now and see how bad it is. When the mess is sorted, Ben can do some internet shopping. Find us a new scanner, new crosscut shredder, and a couple of safe deposit boxes at the bank. From now on we will only keep electronic files in the office and will deposit all papers with personal info at the bank after work."

"Is that practical?" Sabrina asked.

"I do have a personal assistant." Mitzy grinned at Sabrina, but it felt forced, so she shrugged. "We're a one Realtor firm. We can do better than this to keep our clients' identities secure."

"Yeah. It probably was ID theft. Or at least attempted ID theft. Let's get this sorted. You'll probably have to offer all your clients identity protection for a year or something like that." Ben stared at the paper mess. He shifted from foot to foot, a look of uneasiness passing over his features.

"That's probably true." Mitzy scrunched her face up. Her life seemed to be one long attempt to sweep up messes. "Sabrina, when we are done and know the extent of the exposure, please call our insurance agent and see what we can work out."

"Can do." Sabrina scooped up a pile of papers from the brown indoor-outdoor carpet and dropped them on her desk.

That afternoon the interested party for the 72nd house contacted them again. The Realtor was beyond apologetic.

"They had their baby! It was such a surprise. Two weeks early. They didn't know she'd come that morning and totally, in the excitement, didn't even think to call me. But you know, they are out of the hospital now and happy and safe and ready to move. Do you think your seller would reconsider? Have a little grace?" She was begging, really begging.

Mitzy had a number of questions. Her friends were right. As much as she and the Smythes loved the house on 72nd street, a family with cash could get many much better homes right now, for about the same price.

"Dead set on this house, huh?" Mitzy asked, callously ignoring the baby story, which in the back of her mind rang out as untrue.

"Absolutely. They just love the homey neighborhood and want to raise a family there."

Mitzy could hear the smile in the Realtor's voice. She sounded professional. But she also sounded a little like she was lying.

"Really? It's got fairly significant traffic and no nearby parks. I would think they could get something much more family friendly somewhere else." Mitzy wondered if the Realtor would take the bait. The situation with the house wasn't that dire. In truth there was a park a long walk/short drive away. But not necessarily 'near.'

"Oh, I know, Mitzy, I know. But you know how people get when the find 'the one.' I believe he works, or has a number of clients around this area. Something like that and if you have a good reason to live in that part of town, then 72nd is a pretty family friendly area." Her voice was getting a little tenser.

"Indeed. Of course. If it's the one, it's the one, isn't it? She probably already has the kitchen unpacked in her mind. I am going to talk to the sellers, but I tell you what, they are going to want it a little different this time. I will be there for one thing, the whole time. Buyer's closing and seller's closing. They will pick the location. And between you and me, whatever the buyers want they get."

"Within reason, Mitzy."

"I think you will find us reasonable, but it will be at their time and in their time. No more next-thing-in-the-morning business. And before I let you go, I want every number possible for getting in touch with you. We aren't having anyone disappear off of the face of the earth this time."

Which is exactly what Mitzy assumed would happen. Her plan this time was to be present, with her brother, representing her client. They were going to find out what the scheme was and nail the criminals.

She sighed.

She was getting tired of hunting for criminals.

What would she really like to ask these frustrating so-called buyers to do for her?

House Hunters.

The day had been long, depressing, and slow for the whole team and the spring evenings got dark quickly. They spent most of it cleaning papers and trying to get a sense of calm and ownership back, but it hadn't worked well.

They hadn't heard from Joan in a few days.

Ben had taken off for home at lunch.

Mitzy wanted to get Gilbert from her mom's house before she went home. Her mom was pretty in love with the fuzz ball, but Mitzy was thinking she'd like to keep him herself. She said her goodbyes and left Sabrina at the desk.

Sabrina had been thinking a great deal about the housing market. She wasn't completely penniless. And the rumors of awesome houses going for a song had started to get to her.

She was digging deep into the multiple listing service to find herself a home. It was a great time to invest and frankly, with the gala over there was nothing else to do. She looked at the stacks of sorted papers that crowded her desk. No other happy work, at any rate.

She read well past her working hours. It was almost eight when she left the office. The street was deserted. She had driven, but her car was parked around back by the stoneworks. She smiled to herself, a lot of big manly men worked at the stoneworks.

The parking lot was dark.

She squinted into the distance as she turned the corner.

A light was still on at the stoneworks office, but she doubted anyone there could see her.

She turned towards her car and something hit her on the head, a quick thump, hard like iron.

She fell sideways into the building wall.

Her hands flew to her head, but she pulled herself together fast. Her car key was clutched between her fist and her thumb and she jabbed it out towards the attacker's face.

She felt her wrist twist where the attacker grabbed her.

"Help!" she screamed as loud as she could.

The attacker dropped her wrist and grabbed for her laptop case.

She let it drop. "Help!" she yelled louder.

She stomped the bridge of his foot as hard as she could.

He jerked back, but bent down to grab the laptop.

She kneed him in the chin as he looked up.

He looked over her shoulder, turned and ran.

She looked behind her.

Bruce was running across the parking lot about as fast as a man who lifted rocks for a living could be expected to.

He had his cell phone to his ears.

Sabrina hoped he was on the phone with the cops.

He stopped, panting for breath, when he got to Sabrina.

"Are you okay?" He grabbed her by the shoulders and sort of shook her as he took a good look at her.

"I—I'm not sure." She wished he wouldn't shake her. Her head really hurt. She put her hands up to her head and he seemed to get the point.

"I called the cops, do you need an ambulance?"

"My head, where he hit me…and my wrist." She held up her wrist which was red from the twisting.

He put his thick, strong, arm around her shoulders and led her down to the office in the shop. "Come on, kiddo," he said, even though they were about the same age. You need to sit down."

She sat in the stoneworks office, drank the glass of water he gave her and waited, trying desperately to think of a description for the attacker. She pictured herself jabbing at him with her key, but all she could see was his fist twisting her arm.

She remembered his shoe as she stomped on it and his back as he ran away. It wasn't much.

After she made her report, Bruce took her to the urgent care clinic and hung out with her until she had her pain pills and orders to rest at home. Then he took her home.

She lay down on the couch and Bruce stayed with her, pacing awkwardly in the kitchen until her dad showed up. He wasn't going to see her left alone. He shook hands with her father, accepted his thanks and left with very few words.

Sabrina stayed home the next morning. The office was quiet without her. Her innocuous chatter and constant typing were sorely missed as Ben and Mitzy considered the newest problem.

Foreclosed

They sat with their own thoughts, only interrupted by the phone calls from radio listeners, which were few this morning. People had been disturbed, disheartened to hear about Sabrina's incident.

Sad, low down Mitzy on the radio was not the crowd pleaser that up beat or on fire Mitzy was. And there was no way around it—her friend getting mugged for a laptop behind the office made her sad.

After a long measure of silence she spoke again. "But what possible use would someone have for Sabrina's laptop? And how would they know she had it?" She held her coffee cup up to her mouth and let the warmth attempt to comfort her.

"Tweekers," Ben said.

"Really?"

"Probably. Homeless drug users down by the river. They just grabbed the first thing they saw. She doesn't need to bring her laptop here anyway. I don't know why she does it." Ben was slouching in his chair, doing nothing.

"She didn't think he was homeless," Mitzy said.

"She didn't really get a good look at him. 'He' could have been a 'her' for all Sabrina knows. I shouldn't have gone home at lunch. She would never have stayed so late if I had been here to kick her butt out of her chair."

"Don't beat yourself up. How could we know she'd stay late? And why should we have expected someone to be lurking around? Tabby has never been messed with, neither have I, or the receptionist at the music studio."

"I'd like to see the man who'd mess with you or Denise at Music Mania." Ben snorted. He was a good four inches shorter than Mitzy. And Denise was a woman that no one would mess with, in general. She'd have made a great school secretary.

"Do you think it might not be a coincidence?" Mitzy kept an eye on the front window, looking for any sign of trouble on her busy street.

"Do you have a crack pot theory?" Ben asked in return.

"Not crack pot. But someone broke into Brett's house, the museum, and this office. Someone burnt up my rental, and now Sabrina has been mugged."

"Who did you insult at that gala, girl? If that's all related, you've been causing some trouble."

"I didn't insult anybody. But I have been threatening Laurence Mills on the radio. What if he's behind all of this?"

"And what if he's the missing cash buyer?"

"Don't be ridiculous."

"Why not? It's kept you distracted, hasn't it? You want to get a hold of that guy but when was the last time you had any time to do serious spy work? Between missing buyers, talking to cops and your little foray into HGTV land."

Ben was making fun of her, but he was also making her think. And at the moment she thought he was stupid.

"Yes, Laurence Mills who can't afford to keep his own house has gotten me a gig on House Hunters so that I won't have time to um…get him a good price on the property he needs to unload? Interesting theory."

"Or, he has been putting extra effort into keeping you from finding him and making a precedent of his case, getting him hefty fines and possibly jail time into the bargain. I'm sure selling his house from under him only adds insult to the injury."

"Okay, so I haven't been acting with a completely generous spirit. I still wonder how well he knew the folks he bought the house from. That Maxim fellow. He seems much more likely to have a hand in this." She had been chewing on the link between the previous owner and the missing jewelry for a while now. A name like Mikhaylichenko showing up twice couldn't be an accident.

"Are you making a comment about Russians, Mitzy?"

"I'm making a comment about someone who has the same last name as some famous and now stolen jewels."

"So now all Russians are thieves?" he asked, baiting her.

"I think I preferred the deafening silence, thank you." It was a good thing Ben was a talented graphic designer, because in all other respects, he was a real pain.

They sat in silence for quite a bit longer, Mitzy mindlessly scrolling through the multiple listing service and thinking about her troubles and Ben playing minesweeper.

Mitzy saw Bruce through the front window. She waved him in.

"Hey," he said.

"It's good to see you, Bruce." She had never thought of Bruce as a gentle giant before, but after yesterday he seemed something of that sort. A gentle giant meets Clint Eastwood's silent Man with No Name. "I don't know what we would have all done if you hadn't heard Sabrina yesterday. I really can't thank you enough for saving her like that."

"No prob."

"I know her parents were really grateful as well. They called me this morning and told me the whole story."

Mitzy knew she was gushing but she felt that way, so that's the way it was.

"So," Bruce began but took his time getting the rest of the thought out. "I've seen this guy around. I think I know who he is."

"You do?!" Mitzy was amazed.

"Yeah."

Ben even turned in his chair to join the conversation.

"I'm going down to the station to do an ID. But I don't think they've got him."

"Why don't you think so?" Ben asked.

Bruce shrugged, then said, "Just call over if you see a black Nissan pickup parked around here. If you girls are alone, and you see the pickup, just call down to us, okay?"

Mitzy nodded her head vigorously. "Thanks, Bruce, really. Is there anything else I should know? Who do you think it is?"

Bruce shrugged again and left.

Ben swiveled back to his computer, his manhood wounded by the idea that he wasn't man enough to protect the office. He'd be watching monster trucks tonight, that was for sure.

Foreclosed

And now Mitzy had to wonder, why did Bruce know who the attacker was and she didn't? She felt as though she was getting careless.

The rest of the day was long and tense. She couldn't find anyone interested in buying a house on House Hunters. What she really needed was someone just a couple of weeks from closing on their house who'd go on TV and pick it again. Someone who owed her something.

She was back to the cash buyers.

She wondered how they would feel about going on TV. She called the contact numbers for the Realtor and got the busy signal, again and again and again.

Ridiculous.

She Googled the Realtor's name with 'complaints' and got nothing.

Maybe it was time for someone to make a complaint about this lady. The Realtor had very little web presence, but she did find a local White Pages listing with her name. Mitzy wrote the address down and decided it was time to go for a drive.

The address she had found was across town, but traffic was good. She drove fast and made good time. She wasn't familiar with this side of town so she paid close attention to the Google map she had printed. She meandered through a mixed use neighborhood.

There were a number of apartment buildings and some very rundown ranch homes. She drove past two half empty and dreadfully dilapidated mini-malls. One boasted an off brand cigarette and beer type 'grocery store' as an anchor and the other was lacking an anchor all together, but had a payday loan place and an 'adult and family' movie rental place. Not the best part of the city. Not where a successful Realtor would be living.

She began to feel sorry for her professional peer instead of mad at her. She ought to help her out of her misery, teach her a few things. She couldn't help it if her client was a flake, or a fraud or a criminal. But someone ought to help her learn how to tell the difference.

Mitzy was on the right street now. It wasn't a completely worthless neighborhood. The homes were probably fairly nice about twenty years ago. They had just had fallen into the rental trap. There were too many cars parked per home and an air of temporary about them all. More than one home had sheets in the windows instead of curtains and two had for rent signs out front. Mitzy pulled her little Miata into the home with the right house number.

The rain had turned into a soaking mist, but she got out of the car, stood on the unsheltered front step and gave the knocker a few hard raps.

A very small, elderly woman answered the door. She looked sweet.

"Is Helen Berry available?" Mitzy asked gently.

"This is she," the sweet little lady chirped.

"I see." Mitzy tried to keep smiling. "I don't suppose you are Helen Berry, the Realtor I spoke to recently?"

"Goodness no," the sweet little lady said.

"You wouldn't happen to have a daughter who is in real estate?" she asked, grasping for straws.

"No, my dear, I do not. Is there anything else I can do for you? It's a bit drafty in the door." The poor lady was shivering in a house coat and slippers.

"Not at all. Thank you for your time. I'm sorry for bothering you." Mitzy nodded goodbye and returned to her car. Obviously she had the wrong Helen Berry, but had there ever been another one?

Before she drove off, Mitzy used her Blackberry to Google Helen Berry in Portland and again, this address was the only one which came up.

The whole thing was giving her a headache.

Curt liked the idea. Buying a house for cash was kind of fun and unusual. Viewers also liked watching families with new babies find their perfect house. He was all over it, in fact, and got a hold of the elusive Helen Berry himself.

It impressed Mitzy all over again with the power of media.

Curt secured a meeting for all of them in neutral territory, at a Starbucks. They dominated the little seating area in the back with the sofa and arm chairs, in hopes of privacy and comfort.

The couple was striking, Curt thought. Perfect for TV. The baby was brand new, so she'd be the perfect chubby coo-ing age for the follow up shots at the end of the show.

He liked them. He even found the new dad's heavy Russian accent perfect. Anything out of the ordinary way made for a good show.

Mitzy was very wary.

Helen Berry was a short, blond, middle-aged lady in a business suit and sneakers who seemed to be a legitimate buyer's representative.

The missing cash buyers had appeared at last, but they made her incredibly suspicious.

They were at most twenty-five years old and very obviously from Eastern Europe. They had heavy accents, bright blue eyes, and Roman noses. The young mom's hair was up in a bun and she was wearing a long denim skirt.

They drove a two door Acura and wore leather jackets. The wife shifted in her seat and kept her eye on her baby

All Mitzy could think about as she spoke with Martin and Katya were her Romanov-Mikhaylichenko Victorian Mansion-Missing jewel-troubles. She tried not to think of Martin and Katya as a plant by her mysterious nemesis. She tried to get them excited about buying a house via a television show. But it wasn't working.

Curt had his charm on high velocity, but that wasn't working either.

"Tell me what you love about this house," he requested. He leaned forward, his elbows on the table.

"It is very nice," Katya said.

"Great," Curt said. "What is nice about it?"

"It has a big kitchen and very nice yard," Katya responded again. Martin stared hard at Helen, arms crossed on his chest.

"What is the kitchen like?" Curt asked.

"It has…a nice order." Katya worked her jaw back and forth as though she had struggled for the right words.

"You like the layout?" Curt suggested.

"Yes," she said.

"That's great. So when you go on the show, try to talk about all the things you want in your kitchen, and as we look at other houses, you can compare and contrast the kitchens, okay?"

Martin turned his stare to Curt. "We aren't so sure," he said.

"Don't let the cameras make you nervous," Curt said. "You'll get used to them very quickly. Just ignore them—pretend they aren't there. Everyone forgets about them after the first few minutes." Curt nodded while he spoke.

Martin stared at Helen again.

"Purchasing the home via the show is the seller's requirement, Mitzy? That doesn't seem reasonable." Helen laughed, a high, nervous sound.

"You know how people are about their homes, Helen," Mitzy said with a chuckle. "They heard they had a chance to see their home on House Hunters and they just couldn't pass it up. Really, they would rather have it on the show than get it sold fast."

"We do not want to be notorious," Martin said with some heat. He looked from side to side.

"I think he means...celebrities. Is that what you mean, Martin?" Helen suggested with a crooked smile.

"We don't want people...watching what we are doing," Katya said, her eyes fixed on her baby.

Curt looked to Mitzy but she just shrugged. Notorious people who want to keep what they are doing quiet didn't really calm her suspicions.

Helen spoke quietly to her clients in Russian for a few moments.

Curt and Mitzy attempted to discuss other aspects of the show.

Martin cleared his throat. "Katya wants me to build her a house," he said. "We are changing our minds about this house."

While the young couple gathered their jackets and the baby in her car seat, Helen apologized to Mitzy. "I am so sorry to have taken up so much of your time. Young people really are hard to pin down. I thought this was such a great opportunity for your sellers. But I guess if they insist on making a show of their house they will have to find buyers with money and a bit of…a show business kind of attitude." She shook hands absently with Mitzy and followed her clients out.

"Curt, I think we've been had. I think someone has been trying to keep me busy. But I am not going to let it keep happening."

"These guys sure have been pulling you around. Couldn't tell you why myself. But if you run across another rich couple with as much screen appeal let me know right away. That is totally the show I want to produce."

Mitzy left the coffee shop convinced that the couple was related to the jewels and the break-ins. The timing was off though. Their first call had come before the auction.

She tried to piece her last weeks together. What had happened right before she got the call about the house?

Foreclosed

Chapter Eleven

Ben was still seething about Bruce's implications on his manhood. Who was this Bruce character to imply that Ben couldn't look after his women?

Ridiculous.

So he used computers as an artist—strike that—as a designer—as an engineer (better though not quite accurate) instead of playing with rocks all day. Probably Bruce never had a Nintendo when he was a kid and got used to playing with rocks all day. That didn't mean Bruce was manly and Ben wasn't. Ben had to leave work early that day. He had a hair appointment. But none of his thinking was making him feel better. Now was the time for action.

Foreclosed

Ben was yet again alone in the office, so there wasn't much protecting to be done.

Mostly just dusting.

And vacuuming.

He vacuumed like a man, with lots of grunting and banging.

Then he swept the front step, sort of futile in the rain, but he did it anyway. He swept the front of the whole block.

He didn't see anyone from the music studio out in the rain keeping an eye on things.

He scanned the road up and down and didn't see any black pickups.

Bruce was probably fabricating the whole thing.

Bruce the hero, who mysteriously knew who the bad guy was. Bruce the hero, who had mysterious clues about mystery trucks. Stupid Bruce.

Ben went back to the office, put his broom away and took a seat at Sabrina's desk. He could see quite a stretch of parking lot and street from the reception desk. Nothing much was happening, but if any black trucks came by, Ben would know well before Bruce did.

Bruce was eating a meatball sandwich and thinking.

He had been to the ID. He was right. They did not have the suspect and didn't really have a clue who the suspect was. The cops were disappointed.

They had caught a guy running in the general area with the same colored jacket. The guy they caught happened to have a rap sheet. It was win-win as far as the cops were concerned. But he wasn't the right guy.

Bruce had seen him clearly, and knew exactly who he was. He told the cops who they were looking for but didn't figure it would help much.

He tossed the sandwich wrapper across the room into the waste basket.

He was pretty well useless in this fight himself, but someone ought to be looking out for Mitzy and Sabrina, poor kids.

What about that guy on the radio, Johnny? He seemed to be vested in Mitzy. But no, he was a sorry excuse for a man. He'd be worse than useless. Bruce wanted a man of action who knew people.

He thought of Brett, the lawyer brother Mitzy talked about. But he seemed too important and likely to know the wrong people.

Bruce wanted someone who knew people in the building trades who could keep their eyes out for their man.

The attacker was likely to be hanging around, trying to get work but under a different name. He wasn't a man with a lot of friends left, but he only had one skill to fall back on.

Renovations.

He was bound to be looking for work, just not with the people he'd worked for in the past.

Bruce needed to call his buddy Alonzo. Alonzo would know if Laurence Mills was hunting for work, and where. If Alonzo couldn't find the man who mugged Sabrina, no one could.

Ben found himself alternating between the sky-cam traffic cameras on his computer, watching the nearest freeway exits and watching the street.

There was nothing else to do anyway, he told himself.

There it was! No—that wasn't a Nissan. It was a Toyota, and a navy one. He was looking for a black Nissan.

Maybe the bum wouldn't come back. But maybe…maybe he hadn't gotten what he was after.

Ben's eyes flicked back and forth. He thought he saw a black Nissan stopped just off of the freeway exit. He watched to see where it turned.

He lost it in the sea of traffic lights and turned his eyes back to the front window. That particular truck might not have been a Nissan and it might not have been black, though he thought it was. But it had been headed straight which meant in less than five minutes, it would be pulling past. He started another game of minesweeper while he waited.

Before he had emptied his coffee cup, but after two losses and one win (expert level), he saw his man. Not as big as he had seemed (in his imagination, since he hadn't actually been there), but short sandy hair, broad shoulders. From the profile, the man was sort of effeminate.

Ben snickered. Bruce couldn't catch this girly man. But what had made him (if it was really the same guy) come back?

Ben only half believed what he was seeing when the truck pulled into their parking lot.

His heart thundered in his chest and his palms were sweaty. For a moment he thought he was going to puke. He took a deep breath, stood up, squared his shoulders and thought—*Oh crap, what am I doing?!*

He stood in his doorway and tried to look intimidating. The truck had parked just in front of the ceramics studio. Ben couldn't see inside of it from this angle, so he opened the door (slowly) and stepped out.

The driver was just exiting the car.

A surge of adrenaline flooded Ben. He ran up behind the driver and grabbed for him.

Then he felt a blinding pain in his eye. His hand flew to his face as a knee drove into his chest. As he doubled over his foot was crushed beneath a heavy foot.

Ben wobbled and got a knee to his stomach. As he fell over he heard a woman screaming, "Help! Help!"

He tried to stand up, but found it difficult. His hands were over his eyes and he was on his knees panting.

"This man tried to attack me!" a frenzied female voice cried out.

"What?!" Tabby asked incredulously. "Ben? What on earth are you doing on the ground?"

"Black truck—" was all he managed to get out.

"Are you hurt?" Tabby asked.

"Ye-es," he whimpered.

"Not you," Tabby said sharply. "Maggie, are you hurt? Is the rest of your party on the way? Do you want to postpone your painting party or are you going to be okay?"

"I think I'm okay, but I'm going to call the police. That young man ran up right behind me and grabbed me by the shoulders. I think he wanted to mug me."

"I don't think so. This is my friend Ben. I think he has MADE A TERRIBLE MISTAKE and wants to APOLOGIZE RIGHT NOW."

Ben sat up more fully, one hand over his eye still. "I am so sorry, ma'am. I am so sorry. I—we—well—my friend was, was attacked here by someone in a in a black truck and, and…"

"And I look like some kind of attacker to you? Thank you so much. Thank you so very much. Tabby. I need a coffee. I'll be right back." She huffed off across the parking lot to Bean Me Up Scotty's.

"Ben, you're a right idiot, did you know that?"

"She looks like a dude."

"No, she does not. Don't be an idiot. Let me see your eye." Tabby pulled Ben's hand off his eye and looked close. "She got you good, must have been her key. But it was kind of off to the side and didn't poke any holes. I think it will be black though. Very manly. What else did she do, get you in the boys?" Tabby was laughing pretty loud.

He stood up (slowly) and shook himself off. "All right. I'm fine." He limped back to his office and nursed his wounds, both physical and psychological, with another cuppa and some quality time with his Facebook friends.

"Get your courage together. I have a job for us." Mitzy stood in Sabrina's living room, her hands on her hips. She exuded a confidence she didn't exactly feel, but knew that Sabrina needed.

Sabrina was lying on her living room sofa still nursing her new found sense of fear and insecurity. Mitzy wasn't going to let her keep doing it.

"Let me guess, karate lessons?"

"Not at all. We need to go have a chat with a sweet old lady." Mitzy took Sabrina's long wool jacket out of the closet. "Go put something on that looks fabulous with this jacket. Our sweet old lady is rich and expects us to be dressed for tea."

Sabrina rolled over, her back to the television.

"Don't say no."

"I didn't say anything," Sabrina mumbled.

"Do you have a long skirt? If not wool slacks will work." Mitzy let herself into the bedroom and started rummaging through the closet.

"Where is your cream silk blouse? The one with the pearls at the neckline? Wear that one."

"It's at the cleaners," Sabrina called from the couch.

"No, it's right here. You know that I'll drag you up myself, right? We've only got half an hour to get there. Wear your glasses. They make you look smart."

Sabrina dragged herself off the couch and slumped onto her bed. "Why should I go have tea with an old lady?"

"Because this old lady is greatly interested in the missing jewels. And because when I called her and asked her nicely if we could talk about a property that used to be in her family, she kindly invited us over to tea." Mitzy tossed the blouse and a pair of tan slacks to her friend. "Get dressed quick." Mitzy went back to the living room and waited.

Despite her strong inclination to bury herself in her blankets and never come out again, Sabrina found that Mitzy made a compelling case for having tea. And of course, she was Sabrina's boss.

Mrs. Evangeline Simonite-Wilber had the tea table laid in the formal sitting room of her large Craftsman home on the Westside. Mitzy took note of the immaculate woodwork and the original features, such as the buzzers near the door frames to summon the help. The house was three thousand square feet if it was an inch and she was almost certain that there would be a ballroom on the top floor. The whole street was lined with venerable mansions of a by gone era.

Mrs. Wilber, or Evy as she asked to be called, was every bit as chatty and pleasant as she had been at the gala.

"Aren't you young things sweet to come and have tea with me? I was just tickled when you called about the old house in East County. I haven't thought about it in ages." Evy sat in a velvet wing back chair pulled up to the tea table. "Did you know that part of town used to be countryside? Many families had their summer cottages out that way." She said 'families' in a way that left no questions in your mind that she meant important families who had parts of town named after them.

"I was so sad to see it going into foreclosure." Mitzy sipped her tea.

"That is sad. People seem so careless with their property these days." Evy tut-tutted in a mother hen sort of way. "In my day one did not lose one's property."

"It is such a great old house. It could use some fixing up though. I thought it would make a neat bed and breakfast," Sabrina said.

"Oh, you're probably right. It's certainly big enough. I haven't been in it in years. You girls probably weren't even born yet the last time I was in that old pile."

"Old pile? Did the family not keep it up well?" Mitzy asked casually.

"It's certainly a big old house, and I don't remember that that family had enough money to keep it up. It seemed like there was never enough staff and things always looked a bit down at the heels. It is on the Eastside though. I don't imagine one could expect anything else."

Sabrina's back stiffened. Her family had been East-siders for generations. Mitzy kicked her shin under the table cloth.

"I wonder that it got out of the family in the first place," Mitzy mused quietly. She was eager to find out if the 'family' knew anything about Laurence Mills. Or about Maxim Mikhaylichenko.

"It wasn't exactly a family place," Evy said sharply. "Aunty Irene was related to someone who lived there, but I don't think we were. It was always thought of as a bit of a strange place." Evy's back stiffened, ever so slightly. She shifted her shoulders back and her chin out and passed a tray of scones to Sabrina.

"Not family? I'm sorry. I thought I had heard that it was related in some way to the family that donated the jewels to the museum…" Mitzy trailed off.

She didn't know much about Evangeline Simonite-Wilber. She knew that she wanted her old family jewels back. She knew that when she had called asking about the old house, she had casually mentioned the stolen jewels and was invited to tea.

She didn't know how old Evy was or if she was suffering from any kind of dementia. She didn't know how far to trust any information she was gathering. And she didn't know what good the information would do her once she had gathered it.

"Oh, I suppose they were some kind of relation, but it is all so far back. You know, I never knew Aunty Irene. She was mother's aunty. She had all those jewels and gave them all away. She was a princess you know."

"Really?" Sabrina set her cup down and leaned forward.

"Oh yes. She was a Russian princess. Her father immigrated when he lost his lands. I think he lost his lands. You know over in Russia you must have lands if you want to live comfortably. But it might have been his home in town that he lost. I remember a story about a fire."

"Your aunty was a princess who lost her property to a fire?" Sabrina's eyes were wide. "How romantic and Tolstoyian."

"Tolstoyian? Maybe so. Maybe I was remembering a book." Evy held her small, white fist to her mouth and cleared her throat. "There was a fire though, and the family wasn't able to fully recover, so they immigrated to America. I think they came out by way of Alaska." Evy seemed to be gazing at the wall behind Mitzy. "That seems right. They were in Alaska for a while before they came here. I think Aunty Irene had the jewels and had to pass them off to her nieces and nephews. She never had her own children you know. And she never learned English, I'm sure of that."

"She must have been so lonely." Mitzy tried to steal a glance at the wall that held Evy's gaze. Several oil portraits hung over a low bookcase. Was Evy thinking of the people, or the stories?

"Oh, rather not, I'd think. We're a big family. I think some of them somewhere still speak the language. Funny thing that, probably all sorts of new money folks are related to us and don't even know it." She smiled, but only with her thin lips. Her watery blue eyes were hooded.

"New money?" Mitzy asked.

"Oh, probably. I really don't keep up with those people. My charities take up so much of my time you know. That museum, now that is something." Evy began to ramble on about the museum and the jewelry collection and how the women in her family had always wanted to get back their jewelry, but considered it quite impossible.

"Were you terribly disappointed to not get it in the auction?" Mitzy asked.

"Indeed. I had intended to buy it from Ms. Flint-Neuhaus privately after the auction. You can only imagine my disappointment when I heard that it had been stolen." She sighed and her thin shoulders shuddered. A real sadness suffused her features.

"It is a great loss. I hope that they can retrieve it quickly," Mitzy said.

"I'm afraid that the piece will be broken up and the jewels themselves sold. I'm sure they are lost forever now. If mother had known this would happen she would have gotten them back herself."

"Did no one ever try to get the jewels back?" Sabrina asked.

"Never. My husband would say things at times about people and treasure and the lost treasure. You know he has always been a very important man. I think he did a lot to help my family many years ago."

"What kind of help did your family need?" Mitzy was getting lost in the rambling memories and fishing for a straight narrative.

"You must be too young to remember the Cold War. If you had had family behind the Iron Curtain you would know the kind of help they might need."

"That is serious." Mitzy took a sip of her tea. "Your husband must be very important if he was able to get people out of that tyranny." She took a stab at the kind of help a stateside family member might have offered.

Evy gave Mitzy a sharp look. "I suppose those days are gone now, but there was a time when one couldn't speak of these things in such specific terms."

"Do you keep in touch with anyone that your husband helped?" Mitzy asked.

Evy added cream to her tea cup and didn't look up again for a moment. When she did, her face was grim. "Goodness no. We don't keep up with the kind of people who lose their homes to foreclosure. That is irresponsible. Especially after all the help they were given to get here."

Mitzy and Sabrina exchanged a meaningful look.

"Was Princess Irena beautiful?" Sabrina asked, ready as ever to soothe a tense moment.

The rest of the tea was spent looking at pictures of the Simonite women who had longed for their jewels.

Mitzy and Sabrina left with the impression that a great lady felt she had done the poor children a favor and that they ought not to expect to be invited again.

As they drove away they discussed the conversation. Both wondered: When Mrs. Wilber referred to 'new money,' and 'the kind of people who have lost their homes to foreclosure,' was she referring to the Baltimore house going into foreclosure? Was she telling them that Laurence Mills was her family from the old country? Were the Mikhaylichenko-Romanov jewels Mills' family heirlooms as well as Mrs. Wilber's?

Foreclosed

Chapter Twelve

Alonzo couldn't believe what he had been hearing on the radio. Brett Neuhaus' work load must be suffering from the economic crisis like everyone else. Imagine that big shot political hopeful trying a case on the radio. That was all he was doing. Throwing around his political and legal weight, with no real possibility of setting precedent.

Mitzy had talked the lawsuit up like she was going to change the world and then Sabrina was mugged. Today he could hear a change in her voice. She was wearing thin. She didn't have the oomph inside her to tackle the whole economy single handedly. She didn't even have the energy to fight one specific and nefarious enemy, as it appeared she suddenly had.

If Mitzy didn't realize the attack on Sabrina was directly related to her own big mouth, she was a bigger fool than he had thought before.

Foreclosed

While trying to decide if Mitzy was dumber than most blondes, Bruce called.

Mitzy had gotten Sabrina back to the office, but it hadn't helped anyone feel better.

Sabrina was glum and Ben was acting weird. Getting beat down by a middle-aged ceramics painting enthusiast had put him in a terrible mood.

"Can I delete the security pictures yet?" Sabrina asked as she scrolled through the pictures on her phone.

"Sure," Mitzy said.

"What security pictures?" Ben asked with an edge to his voice.

"From Aerin's office," Sabrina said.

"Why do you have security pictures from Aerin's office?" Ben leaned forward to look at Sabrina's phone with her.

"It seemed like a good idea at the time," Mitzy said.

"A good idea for what?" Ben asked. "Are those museum security camera shots?"

"Yes."

"How did you get those?"

"We went to visit Aerin, okay?" Mitzy didn't appreciate the insolent interrogation.

"And she thought it was a good idea for you to take pictures of what? The robbery?" He squinted at the blurry images of the masked man.

"We didn't ask," Sabrina said, as she hit delete.

"How did you get classified pics without asking?"

"I don't think you want to know." Mitzy closed her email and turned to look at Ben.

"If you were playing spy, I hope no one saw you." Ben shook his head.

"Do you think that one guy knew what we were doing?" Sabrina asked Mitzy.

"Why would he?" Mitzy tapped her fingers on her knee, a nervous gesture that didn't help her calm down.

"He saw us. He saw the camera. Maybe he guessed."

"Wait a second. Dude. Someone saw you all hanging over Aerin's desk with a camera? Do you know who it was?"

"No. We didn't know him and he didn't know us," Mitzy said.

"Can you be sure?" Ben asked.

"Why would it matter? Why should we worry about the janitor?" Sabrina's eyes were huge.

"You did just get your laptop stolen. We were wondering why someone was after your computer." Ben sat back. He shook his head in frustration. "There is a chance that sneaking around stealing pictures of a robbery would make someone want to get their hands on your electronics."

"Are you saying the mugging was my fault?" The blood rushed to Mitzy's cheeks.

"I'm not saying anything, Mitzy." Ben's voice had a snide edge that spoke volumes.

Mitzy clipped Gilbert's leash on his little blue collar and left the office. She was angry with Ben, but much angrier at herself.

She had imagined learning a little more about the robbery would keep them safe, not get her best friend hurt.

She got in her car, but then didn't know what to do. Would further spy-like action put them in more danger or help them out of the mess they were in?

Mitzy reached over and patted Gilbert's head. He was so small and dependent. She hadn't yet been able to leave him alone anywhere. She just couldn't. And she couldn't get a hold of Joan.

The rain drummed on the soft top of the Miata. The pressure was like a heavy blanket draped over Mitzy.

Her head and the sky were thundering. Her stomach was boiling. Her jaw was clenched like a vise. As the spring rain pounded over her she watched a pool of water collect at a seam on the roof. The developing leak fascinated her eyes, but didn't register with her mind.

If there was a connection between the robbery at the museum and Sabrina's mugging, then there was a connection between the burnt-out rental, Laurence Mills, the attack, and the missing cash buyers—all of it. The whole tangled affair hinged on one thing, if only she could suss out what that was.

In the back of her mind a voice nagged that Alonzo was behind it. Tears filled her eyes, hot and burning. Why was he torturing her? She was sure things would be different after she had seen him at church on Sunday. A man like that...he shouldn't be able to torture her like this.

She drove to her Baltimore rental and stared at the singed walls of her rental property. Her renters—her friends—were displaced now.

In business she was keen. She had to be that way now. Sharp and attentive. All she had been trying to do for the last week and a half was sell the Victorian on Baltimore. What had happened instead?

First, Alonzo and Carmella decided to try and buy the house and turn it into a commercial property.

Then she had hosted the gala in hopes of finding her own buyer for the house. While there she had seen the now infamous Romanov pendant.

There had also been a handful of crimes: a burglary at the museum and Brett and Aerin's house, and a break-in at the office. Sabrina mugged, but doing fine. The fire at the rental, still being investigated for arson.

There was a bit of real-estate business, the on again-off again buyers and the House Hunters gig.

Then there was Gilbert.

She needed to figure out which pieces fit this puzzle. Despite what she wanted to believe, not all of this could be related.

At the gala, Aerin had won the pendant and then lost it again, which was obviously why both her home and the museum were burgled. They shared the name Neuhaus with Mitzy which could explain the break-in at the office.

Foreclosed

But more likely that the break-in and the mugging were about the pictures she and Sabrina took at the museum. Which meant the man in the hat was somebody important.

Maybe Laurence Mills himself.

Tea with Mrs. Wilber had neatly tied the house and the jewelry together. Princess Irena had lived in the Baltimore house with a collection of jewelry and then given much of it away. It was likely that the house had remained 'in the family' up until it went into foreclosure.

But what did Mitzy know about the family? What did she need to know about the family? Were Alonzo and Carmella related to the Romanov-Mikhaylichenko family?

Mitzy broke from her reverie and started her car. It was time to hit the historical society reading room.

At the reading room, she hunched over her microfiche machine, scanning through property deeds from a hundred years ago. She was looking for the first papers to the land on what is now Baltimore Street and Smith Blvd. It was a long slow process. The deeds were handwritten and Baltic looked like Baltimore as did Marlborough and many other things that could only be read by application of a strong looking glass. She didn't keep one in her purse, but the archivist had one she could borrow.

She had twelve months' worth of records at her station as well as some newspapers to scan through. She searched for the name Romanov and Mikhaylichenko together or otherwise.

When she thought she couldn't take another minute of sitting crouched over the low desk she found her first clue.

The parcel of land that the map would confirm as the one in question was originally deeded to a Mr.....it looked like it might be McCutcheun, but she was just guessing.

The record she had found was a bill of sale. McCutcheun sold it to Mr. Harry Something-or-Other and his wife Mrs. Harry Romanov-Something-or-other in 1899. This was the last thing she had expected to find, but worth noting. She ordered a print of the record.

Since she had a name and a date she to moved on to Google and USGenweb for a little census search.

When did the Romanov-Something-or-Others get to Portland and how long had they been here? And what was the Something-or-Other name in reality? The best she could make of it was Simlington, but that just didn't sound like a name.

She wore out the search and find function on the census record without finding anyone called Simlington or Siml* in her county. They had to have been there of course, she just had the name wrong. So with an aching neck, she moved her hunt to the card catalogue.

The card catalogue was as useful as it had been in high school. She immediately found an article in *Antiquities and Antiques* about the missing Romanov jewels.

After the revolution, a great deal of looting had been done and there was a lengthy catalogue of missing pieces. Adventurers, displaced heirs, and the filthy rich had spent decades trying to find the lost treasures. Of course, many pieces such as the Romanov-Mikhaylichenko piece were legitimately owned by museums. But despite the impeccable, ephemera, these pieces were sought after by collectors of Russian antiques on behalf of the current government of Russia.

They were even more hotly pursued by displaced royalty descended from people who had happened to be out of the country during the revolution.

The Romanov-Mikhaylichenko collection was a little famous in its own way. It had remained in the possession of Princess Irena Mikhaylichenko, a distant relation of the Romanovs who lived in the US. It was thought that she had pieced out the collection as gifts in her old age. The last known piece was the necklace given to the museum by a nephew of Princess Irena.

However, a few living relatives remembered Irena was supposed to have only given away a small part of her family collection. Princess Irena had ended her days in this town living with her niece, on the Romanov side.

Living in the Baltimore Victorian.

Another article came up on the Romanov connection. This one was a local Architectural Magazine from the 1980s. It seemed the Baltimore Victorian had been the baby of a very wealthy Indian Scout who had settled down after the war with his own…princess.

Of course.

His own distant relation to the then royal family of Russia.

They had designed their home to reflect their disparate passions. It had been a showpiece to some and a design disaster to others. At any rate it was eventually forgotten and left to disrepair and old age. This article was written by a local historian with an eye to rehabilitate local landmarks. Other buildings of interest were also discussed. A few of the homes written about Mitzy knew had been made landmarks and restored.

Who knew about Mitzy's rental and her desire to protect its value by getting a family into the empty mansion? Who knew about the jewels and the winning auction bid by Aerin? Who would have been doing a title search and learning about the history of the Victorian? Who was going out of his way to purchase the Victorian even though there were a million places on the market right now? She knew all of that.

And so did Alonzo Miramontes.

He was after the house to find the missing jewels.

She was as sure of it as if she were after them herself. She couldn't put her finger on why he wanted them so badly, but business was bad everywhere and everyone needed money. He must have heard about the jewels from his aunt and uncle well before the auction. And now he was determined to have them.

The key to the jewels that were still missing from the infamous collection was hiding somewhere in the house.

She had to figure it out before he did.

After the attack on Sabrina, she was sure there were no measures he would not take.

Aerin's necklace was gone, and so was Mitzy's rental. Alonzo had to be stopped.

Foreclosed

"She's going to get herself killed," Alonzo muttered. "Poor kid." But she wasn't a poor kid. She was in vital danger.

The Victorian had gone into foreclosure before he could get a short sale on it. Since then he had paid close attention to what Mitzy said on the radio.

The constant threats to Laurence Mills were going to get her in trouble.

Laurence Mills, for all intents and purposes had disappeared. He had looked into his whereabouts, since Bruce had asked him to, but no luck.

And with his fairly nondescript appearance, he was hard to find in a city as big as Portland. Mid-height, broadish shoulders, sandy brown to brown hair. A straight nose. A round, or broad face, or maybe not. Forty or fifty years old. He could be almost anybody anywhere. No one seemed to remember seeing him, at least not for certain.

Ben remembered seeing a man who almost fit that description parked in their parking lot the day the office was ransacked but he couldn't describe the car. It was champagne colored, or tan. It was a jeep or a ford or something like that. Possibly mid '90s. But Bruce knew that was all wrong. They were looking for the black pickup truck. If ever a man defied description it was Laurence Mills. It was like he had intended to disappear. Which he had done very well.

Apparently there was some trouble over the jewelry from the auction as well. Dangerous trouble. Two nights after Mitzy's sister-in-law had won the piece, the museum where it was held was burgled. All of the jewelry was stolen and all but the Romanov piece were found later, abandoned with an abandoned car. It was all evidence now, at the police station. He had heard that Aerin's home had been burgled as well. Alonzo figured the two were connected, that the pendant was the object of both break-ins.

The thing that started him thinking on it this time was Mitzy on the radio. She just wouldn't let up. Today she was talking again about her little assistant Sabrina who had been attacked on her way home from work.

It made Alonzo red-faced angry. Sabrina was innocent. Mitzy and Brett were causing all of the fuss on the radio and in the newspaper.

He had done a title search on the Victorian when he tried to buy it for his sister. It had only had four owners, which was entirely unexpected, considering the age of the place. He assumed that at some point the deed had been transferred to an heir of the same name and it was just recorded incorrectly.

The second owners were Mr. Harry Simonite and his wife who was called Mrs. Harry Romanov-Simonite. The Simonite family built the house that was still there. The home remained in the hands of the Simonites until Maxim Mikhaylichenko bought it from them in 1970. And it stayed in Maxim's name until he sold it to the mysterious Laurence Mills.

Alonzo had had a headache since his car accident, and he blamed Mitzy. It was time for her charade to end. And the best way to end it was at the source. He'd just have to go to the house and see what it was that everyone wanted so bad.

Foreclosed

Chapter Thirteen

Mitzy couldn't take the wondering any more. All the clues she could dig up pointed to a mystery at the house itself. The only way to get to the bottom of it was to go there. Right now.

The house had a lockbox and she had a keycode to open it. She was going to find out what was in hiding on Baltimore Street before Alonzo hurt another person.

She parked in the driveway of her destroyed rental house.

She crept out of her car as quietly and carefully as a woman in stiletto boots wearing a puppy in a frontpack could.

Dusk was falling with its promise of shadows. She wasn't breaking and entering, but she was glad for the coming dark.

Something in Mitzy expected the lock to stick, the door to groan open, and the floor to collapse under her.

Instead, the door opened quietly to the restored foyer she had seen through the windows earlier. The floors glowed like gold in the slanting rays from the setting sun.

The inlaid compass in the center of the floor looked like it was under a spotlight. The entry was as large as some living rooms Mitzy had shown.

The compass.

She tilted her head and looked at it again. It was off. Those windows were dead west but the compass showed them as more southwest. Why would someone craft such a perfect thing wrong? She tapped the toe of her boot on the polished wood, and then went North, by the compass's directions.

Across the perfect floor, two staircases curved around and met at a second story mezzanine.

The north arrow led her to what she would have called the front parlor.

The floors weren't restored in this room. They were scuffed and covered in plaster dust.

One wall, the one they had noticed through the window, had a large hole. The dead black of the hole sent a shiver up Mitzy's spine.

She wrapped her arms around the warm puppy and took a deep breath. She didn't have time to be scared.

Mitzy made her way to the wall.

She dropped to her knees and peered into the hole.

She poked her hand into it, but found only the scratchy edges of horsehair plaster and lath. The hole in the wall was deep—the old house had thick walls. But it was empty.

Mitzy stood up and dusted the knees of her jeans.

The remains of a ceiling medallion clung to the plaster ceiling. She squinted at it. It looked like the rays of a sun, perhaps. She had never seen a design like it before.

The light fixture was gone as was most of the center of the medallion. She stood on her tip toes and reached for the hole, but the ceiling was very high. She couldn't reach the hole, or see inside.

Along the outside wall there was a marble fire place that seemed almost cheery in the empty room,

She gave it a thorough once over. The dust was thick all over it, but there wasn't much inside.

There were ashes, and a cold draft blew down through the chimney.

There were no marks in the dust which was chalky white, even in the dusky half light of the unlit room she could tell it was coated in clean, new construction dust, most likely from damage to the ceiling, and possibly from the walls.

She went back into the foyer, which was still brighter.

Her eyes followed the staircases. The banisters came down to grand posts, shaped like arrows, another design element she had never seen. Her heart fluttered. This was what she had read about in the magazine, the special designs the retired Indian Tracker had insisted on.

Foreclosed

The arrow wasn't straight up and down, but sort of set at an angle. She studied the staircase a bit longer. The smaller posts on the railing were all arrowheads and all at an angle.

She traced the carved arrowhead with her finger. You would never find custom work like this in a modern home. She worked her jaw back and forth to keep from crying. This home deserved better than what it had received from life.

Mitzy followed the arrows up the stairs.

From the mezzanine she scanned the foyer below. The compass was the only thing obviously unusual at the front of the house. And from here, it seemed to be pointing most directly at the base of the staircase and not the formal parlor.

Mitzy turned and gave her attention to the mezzanine.

The woodwork was in disrepair, but she could see the ghost of its former glory in what remained.

Two carpenters who would love to get their tools on it came to mind. She imagined it gleaming and golden. It deserved that.

The mezzanine was like a long hall that stretched the length of the foyer. There were four doors, two to the left of the staircase and two to the right.

Straight back from where the two branches of the stairs met was a large deep room, or sitting area.

The sitting area was flanked with more doors.

She tried to remember how many bedrooms the house was listed as having, but couldn't pin it down.

She walked slowly into the sitting area, taking note of anything out of the ordinary. A huge leaded glass window dominated the back wall, and the skeleton of a deep, long window seat, with built-in book shelves on either side stretched the length of the room. The panels and the bench had been removed from it.

The supporting structure of the seat showed damage, as though the wood had been ripped off with violence. Mitzy's stomach turned. She knew they'd never find the missing pieces.

There was very little furniture in the house, but a buffet or bar of some sort was still in the sitting room. With the view over the back property this must have been a place the Victorians who build the house had loved to sit and entertain. She could imagine the bar filled with shiny bottles and glassware.

She hated to admit it, but the house would make a lovely little inn.

Dark had set in fully now and Mitzy could see the moon from the large window, but it didn't shine brightly enough to light the room.

She pulled a small flashlight from her purse (a Realtor has to be prepared). She wondered if it would be worth it to run back out to her car and grab the Maglite, but decided against it, both because it was so dark out, and because she didn't want to stop.

She pushed open the door to the room closest to her instead. She swept the room with her little flashlight. It was papered in something vintage, possibly original.

From the glow of her flashlight it seemed in good condition. She sighed. If Evy Simonite-Wilber had loved the old jewelry so much, how much more would she love the house, if only she could see it again?

The paper was a toile pattern, but in a Native American design of hills and ponies and tee pees, a deep maroon pattern set against yellowing cream.

She touched it gingerly, just with her fingertips. It wasn't paper, but silk.

The room, true to its era, had no closet but was of a decent size and must have been a bedroom. She was sure it could fit the standard four poster bed, a wash stand and a wardrobe of the era. Those few pieces would fit perfectly and be all that was expected, even in a home of this quality.

The fixtures were missing from the wall—gas light fixtures. There was no switch for electric, so possibly when electric had been added it had been added only for rooms that a smaller family with less money had been using.

She knew just the electrician she would hire if she could buy the house from the bank.

There was a hole in the wall where the gas fixture had been. Mitzy lit it up with her flashlight but there was nothing to see, just thin gas piping.

It would be impossible to clean and restore the silk wall coverings with such a large hole cut out.

What a waste.

The condition of the next room was similar, though there was an electric light switch. Mitzy tried it but wasn't surprised to find it did nothing.

The electricity had surely been turned off when the bank took ownership.

She let her flashlight shine on the walls. They were papered in something from the 1970s; eagles and flags. She looked around for any fixtures, but there were none, though there were wires hanging from the ceiling where an electric light fixture had been previously.

In this room there was no obvious damage. She wondered about the selectivity of the person who had sliced up the house. What did he already know as he tore it apart? Did he have a treasure map or just an eye for what could be resold most easily?

The next bedroom had been stripped bare to the plaster. There was no paper, no silk, no wood trim, no electric outlets or switches and no gas fixtures. The floor was even stripped of its wood, leaving the wide old planks of sub floor exposed. On the other hand, there were no large holes cut into any wall or ceiling or floor and no damage done to what was left behind.

In fact, it looked almost like this room had been cleared quite a few years ago by someone who was careful.

She was learning a bit about the house, but the information so far was scattered and didn't fill any of the holes she had in her story.

She moved on to the rooms across the way, hoping to find something more useful.

The first room had its original toile silk, but this pattern was of an Eastern, or Russian look with thatched roof villages and onion roofed churches.

There were no switches or outlets, so apparently it hadn't been used as a bedroom in the last seventy years. The gas fixtures had been removed, but nothing had been cut up.

Or had it? She swung her light into a dark corner and looked more closely. There was a fairly large hole, but it seemed more like a critter nest than her treasure.

She shook her head. Was she a fool? She was hunting treasure in an old empty house—and expected to find it. The other house hunter was too. They both wanted to find the rest of the lost Mikhaylichenko-Romanov jewels.

But he seemed to have a treasure map, and all she had was her wits.

Her heart beat pounded in her chest.

Why was the compass off of due North and why did the balustrade have arrows? Was she supposed to follow the arrows? The compass led her first to the parlor where the most extensive digging had been done. She surmised the other treasure hunter had followed the arrows there as well.

The staircase arrows led her upstairs, but so far only the rooms on the side where the compass was pointing had been damaged. Another point in favor of the compass being a clue.

Mitzy slipped the door shut quietly and moved on to the next door. It was locked.

Alonzo pulled his pickup truck into the driveway of the Victorian but not all the way to the front. In one upstairs window he saw a spot of light, like a small flashlight. *What on earth does she think she is doing?* He had seen Mitzy's Miata in the driveway next door. *Didn't that burned up house scare her at all?* He turned off his engine shaking his head. It was beyond him how a woman like her could make it in the world. The more he thought about her the more she seemed like a child. An incredibly lucky (and pretty) child.

He had a Realtor's lockbox code as well as she did. So he opened the house and slipped inside.

He was torn between calling out her name so he could get her out of this place fast and sneaking up on her.

He would love to see her jump.

He chuckled, but decided against it.

Knowing a little about the house he stopped to admire the once famous compass. It was set at an odd angle and seemed to point to the stairs, or maybe the parlor, or maybe even to the narrow wall between the two.

The little wall wasn't about two feet wide, not large enough for a closet. He ran his hand over the wall paper and felt something odd, like a panel or a door. He looked up to the mezzanine. There was a straight line of boxed-in space, the whole way up.

Foreclosed

His first thought was disused dumbwaiter, but there was no door at the top, unless it had been papered over as well.

They were on the wrong side of the house for a kitchen dumbwaiter. Perhaps this one led to the laundry. He crossed the foyer and checked the other wall. This wall didn't seem to have anything hiding behind the paper, but it was the same size as the opposite wall and adjacent to the kitchen.

Mitzy was probably safe upstairs for a few more minutes. And anyway, if someone wanted to join the party, he'd hear them come in.

He entered the kitchen and found the door for the right hand dumbwaiter. He figured it probably led from the kitchen up to the ballroom floor just under the servants' hall.

There was no mystery to Alonzo about the destroyed kitchen. A desperate man would do anything he could when everything he owned was on the line. Of course he had sold off the kitchen improvements.

Alonzo walked through the kitchen and into the butler's pantry where things were a little more interesting.

The doors were off of the built-in cabinets and the shelves were stacked against the walls. There was shattered glass on the floor, likely from damage to the glass fronted doors.

There was a large square hole cut in the ceiling above him. He tipped his Maglite up to the ceiling but it didn't help. He hoisted himself up onto the counter and leaned towards the hole. He could almost reach inside of it and could see fairly clearly. The empty space between the upstairs sub floor and the ceiling had been used for hiding something.

Mitzy fished a hairpin out of her handbag. The lock was a hundred years old; surely a hairpin could open it. She fiddled with it for quite sometime, until it finally clicked and she pushed the door open.

The room was packed with antique furniture, full from wall to wall and floor to ceiling.

She stroked the nearest piece. The wood had texture, and history. She wondered if any of it was original to the Romanov Princess.

She flashed her little light all around the room. The light flashed on glass and a pair of bright blue eyes stared out at her. Her heart caught in her throat; it was a moment before she realized it was her own face in a mirror.

The light bounced around from gilded frames to brass drawer knobs, and more small mirrors.

She inched into the room and tried a drawer. With the puppy strapped to her chest there was barely enough room for her to stand between the wall and the furniture.

The drawer she tried slid opened. It was empty.

She would need daylight and a team of strong men to sort through all of this. She inched her way out of the room again and shut the door.

It was full dark in the house now. Her Indiglo watch said it was 9 pm.

All of her nerves were on edge. She tapped a fast staccato with her foot and tried to gather her thoughts. Were the missing Romanov jewels hidden in this house? Jewels that left the old country long before the Romanovs lost their lives? Or had they been given out as gifts by an otherwise impoverished old woman who relied on the kindness of relatives for her living?

Or had that rumor been invented by someone who wanted to keep the jewels a secret?

And what did she know about the house that people who had lived here for generations would not have known? She had to have some advantage or there was no point in being here.

Someone had handled all of the furniture that was locked away. If jewels were hidden in any of the pieces of furniture, it was likely it had been done in the day of the person who lived with the furniture. *Perhaps*, she thought, *this was where the things that had already been searched were being stored*. She had only seen one piece of furniture not in that room—the bar.

She pulled open the drawers and ran her long slender hands over their bottoms. She turned them over and felt their backs, looking for any irregularities. She shined her light into the cavities that held the drawers. She searched every inch of the shelves as well.

Then she ran her hands under the bottom of the piece of furniture.

A long, thin piece of metal was taped to the bottom. She peeled the crinkly tape off, her hands shaking and her breath coming fast.

The metal rod had a circle at one end and was bent a bit at the other. It reminded her of something you'd use to turn the water on in the yard. Like a key. But you wouldn't tape a sprinkler system key to the bottom of a bar.

She needed to get into the basement.

Alonzo found three empty boxes inside the ceiling crawl space. They were fairly old and mouse gnawed. A stack of mouse-chewed papers had spilled across the interior of the plaster ceiling as well.

Alonzo scooped them out and shoved them into his jacket.

He reached as far as he could into the ceiling, and then thought it might be a good idea to get a ladder.

He heard Mitzy running down the stairs. He drummed his fingers on the ceiling. If he could just get the last of this out of the hole before she ran off, he'd call it good.

He hopped to the floor.

Glass shattered at his feet, slicing his shin. Warm blood dripped down his leg.

He had landed on one of the unbroken glass doors, crushing it and slicing his leg in the process. He slipped off his jacket, the papers fluttered to the floor.

He leaned against the cupboard and picked bits of glass out of his leg. He bit his tongue to keep from cursing. He'd find Mitzy in a minute.

Mitzy made her way through the parlor into a sunroom at the back of the house. A door led from there to the cellar. She was on the second step when she heard a crash on the kitchen side of the house.

Foreclosed

She gripped the stair rail. And paused, mid step.

Then she ran down the rest of the stairs, her hand hovering over Gilbert's head.

Alonzo had caught up with her.

At the bottom of the stairs she illuminated the room in small circles.

Dirt floor.

Shelves.

Some stainless steel something or other—oh yes, that was the missing stove.

Pipes.

Bricks.

Legs, in work boots.

"Hello, Mitzy Neuhaus. I see you've made your way to the basement at last."

Alonzo had picked the glass shards from his leg and wrapped the wounds with the lining from his jacket. Forgetting the papers, he limped into the foyer.

Mitzy was long gone.

He hadn't heard the front door open, so he headed to the parlor. But it was empty too, so he went through to the sunroom.

As he looked around he heard the distinctive whine of a small puppy.

A puppy?

Why could he hear a puppy?

He flashed his heavy light back into the parlor.

He wasn't sure where the puppy noises were coming from but it gnawed at him. The house had been closed for a long time, in puppy years. If there was a puppy in here it had to be starving to death.

"It could use a coat of paint. And some new lighting." Mitzy was rigid with fear, dripping with sweat, and seconds from panic.

"What?"

In the moment of pause she had her long, thin metal rod pointed out and up.

She moved her small light around trying to see the whole man. Mid height. Sandy brown, to brownish hair. Round, sort of square face. A low, heavy brow.

"You're not Alonzo." She took a step backwards, towards the stairs. Gilbert was whining. A warm spot developed on her silk blouse.

"Indeed. And you are not where a good girl should be." He lunged forward.

Mitzy jabbed the rod into his chest.

"Ouch!" Even his holler of pain had an accent.

"Are there jewels down here, or just appliances?" Mitzy took another small step backwards, her heels hitting the bottom step.

"Now why would there be jewels in an old dump like this?" he asked with a sneer.

"It depends, I suppose, on if Aunty Irene really gave them all away as gifts or not, doesn't it?" She leveled her key at him. He put his hand to his chest, instinctively.

"Our Great Aunt Irene left it all to her nephew."

"Your Great Aunt Irene?" Mitzy leaned forward to get a better look at him.

He lunged forward, his hands on the puppy sling and dragged her to him and to the ground.

"He's just a puppy!" Mitzy shouted. She kicked but couldn't find him with her feet in the dark.

The nondescript man kicked Mitzy in the stomach.

Tears sprung to her eyes, and bile filled her throat.

She wrapped her arms around the puppy and whispered the prayer of the desperate. "Oh, Lord, please help!"

Alonzo was at the door to the basement in less than a second. He had heard Mitzy cry out.

She had the puppy and someone had her.

He couldn't believe he had missed the door to the basement. Couldn't believe he hadn't gone straight to the cellar to see where the dumbwaiter's shaft ended.

Couldn't believe that someone could actually hurt his Mitzy.

No, not his Mitzy. Just Mitzy.

He bounded down the stairs in three steps and punched whoever that guy was in the head. His knuckles stung with the impact, but the man fell against the wall, so it was worth it.

Mitzy was a crumpled mess on the floor, whiny puppy somewhere in the room with her and her massive pile of blond curls shining in the glow from his flashlight.

"Laurence," Alonzo said.

"Miramontes," Laurence replied.

Mitzy groaned. If Alonzo was here, she was done for.

Alonzo crouched down beside Mitzy and brushed her hair aside.

Laurence Mills grabbed a two by four and swung it at Alonzo's head. It hit.

Joan rang the bell at Mitzy's penthouse. She rang it again. She looked at her watch. It was just after nine. Surely Mitzy wasn't at the office. She sighed. She wanted to collect that sweet puppy. She felt terrible for leaving it for so long. She pressed her ear against the door but couldn't hear anything. She pushed the bell button one more time before giving up.

Joan supposed the puppy was fine. Or maybe Sabrina had it. She wished she had her cell phone on her, but it was charging back home.

She took her van over to Sabrina's and rang the bell.

Foreclosed

Sabrina answered wearing her bathrobe, a wine glass in hand. "Hey, care to join me? I'm watching *House* on Tivo." She motioned for Joan to come in.

"I'm just looking for Gilbert." A glass of wine and some television sounded nice. Especially that charming old Hugh Laurie.

"Mitzy has him. I thought you knew that." Sabrina wandered back into her living room and put the television on pause.

"You know, I thought she did, but she wasn't home so I second guessed myself. Do you know where she went?" Joan played with the moonstone necklace she was wearing.

"I don't. Maybe Brett's to talk about the lawsuit?" She was pouring another glass as she spoke. "I saw you eyeing the good doctor. I know you want to stay." She passed the second glass over to her friend.

Joan accepted the glass, swirled it in the cup, checking out the legs. It wasn't too cheap looking. She sniffed it and took a sip.

"I'm sure the puppy is safe with Mitzy." She followed Sabrina over to the sofa. They put their feet up and let House get back to business.

As Laurence tied Mitzy to the prone figure of Alonzo, it occurred to her that perhaps Alonzo wasn't after her after all. But whatever the circumstances, Mitzy thought it better to act dazed and get tied up, than to go his route and get hit in the head with a big stick.

Alonzo's large, heavy flashlight had rolled to the base of the staircase. Her arms were free at the elbow so she stroked Gilbert, trying to get him to calm down. She didn't want him to draw attention to them and have to take the force of a blow from the man Alonzo had called Laurence.

Laurence didn't seem to realize the importance of the key she had. As she fell she had let it slip gently to the ground beside her, and it was still within reach. Alonzo's big, heavy Maglite, which had turned off when it hit the ground, was very near her toes.

She felt Alonzo pulling at their restraints as he lifted his head. *Idiot*, she thought.

He was struck down again by the treasure hunter.

Laying low was definitely the best option. They weren't tied carefully or tightly, but if Alonzo took too many blows to the head she wouldn't be able to drag him out of the basement as she fought off the bad guy alone.

There was a loud crash from the back of the cellar followed by a long stream of cursing.

Laurence kicked Alonzo in the stomach as he hoofed it out of the basement.

Alonzo groaned.

A moment later, he was whispering to her. "Idiot. You're going to get yourself killed by this lunatic. Do you have any idea who he is?"

"Apparently he is Laurence Mills." She stiffened. Alonzo was still Alonzo, even if he wasn't after the jewels.

"Laurence is Mikhaylichenko and Mikhaylichenko is Russian Mafia, Mitzy. He kills people," Alonzo hissed.

"Funny I didn't see his name in my copy of who's who of the Mafia."

"Don't be a fool, Mitzy. He is a very dangerous man."

"As you have seen for yourself." Mitzy twisted in the rope, trying to gauge how much give it had.

"I'm not tied up here alone, am I?" Alonzo said.

"I suppose you know who Princess Irena Romanov is as well, and exactly how she is related to Laurence Mills." Mitzy was showing off and wriggling the ties loose at the same time.

"Hold still!" Alonzo's whisper sounded angry.

The rope they had been tied with was below her knees already, so she ignored him and kicked it all the way off.

"Do you know where that puppy is? We need to find him." This time Alonzo's whisper had a hint of fear in it.

Mitzy reached over for his hand and pulled it to her dog sling.

"Why are you wearing a dog?" He kept his hand on the puppy's head while he crawled to his knees.

"He is too little for a leash. Are we escaping now or not?" She was ready to sit up when Laurence or Maxim or whoever he was came flying down the stairs again.

He grabbed Alonzo by the shoulder and dragged him to his feet. He must not have been paying very close attention to details as he didn't seem to notice his two captives weren't tied together anymore.

"I am going to pry this loose and you are going to hold it up for me," Laurence or Maxim said.

The sound of a pry bar scraping on stone was all Mitzy heard for a few moments.

Patting the puppy in hopes to keep him quiet, Mitzy inched her way, still lying on her side, to the bottom of the staircase. She wondered how the treasure hunter knew he was at his target in the dark. She slipped the Maglite into her hand and then rose to her knees.

She slowly crossed the cellar, the knees of her wool slacks scraping across the hard packed dirt floor. Then, when she reached the men, she silently rose to her feet.

She raised the Maglite high above her head with one hand and prodded the key into Laurence/Maxim's neck with the other. "Stop!" It was the best she could think of in the moment but she said it loud.

The large stone or whatever it was hit the ground with a thud. The pry bar didn't drop, Mitzy noted.

"Alonzo, call 911!" Mitzy ordered. She could hear him rustling his pockets and hoped he had a phone on him.

"You're too late. You'll be dead and I'll be gone long before any police can make it here."

Mitzy jabbed his neck with her rod.

"Ouch!"

She pushed the key harder into his fleshy neck. "Maxim Mikhaylichenko we know who you are, we know how to say your stupid long last name, and we know you are looking for the jewels. But you won't find them in the storm drain." Mitzy twisted the rod.

Maxim pulled his neck away, but Mitzy kept her rod pressed hard against him.

"You can't kill us because we know exactly where the jewels are and you do not. You need us."

"You seem to be mistaken about my current plan."

"Don't be coy," Mitzy said. "You know I have the drain key pressing your neck right now. But you thought you could just pry it apart. I don't know what you will find in that drain. I'm sure it is interesting. But it's not the jewels, is it, Alonzo?" She was bluffing. Her key was probably the key to the drain and it was probably where the jewels were hidden.

Maxim moved ever so slightly and Mitzy brought the Maglite down on his head. The force shook her to her shoulders.

Maxim's hands flew to his head and he dropped the pry bar. Alonzo grabbed it in an instant and dropped Maxim with one blow to the back of his knees.

"Tell me you found your phone!" Mitzy yelled as she ran for the stairs. Her purse was in the foyer and her cell phone was with it. Alonzo said nothing but stayed with Maxim, who was down, but not out.

She stumbled up the stairs, one hand on the dog and raced to her phone. She couldn't help but wonder if Maxim had a gun.

"Aerin is so mean." Sabrina had had just enough sips of her wine to be chatty. "She's nasty, snooty mean. I hope she's not mean to Gilbert."

"She's too cool to be mean to a puppy." Joan was still sipping her first glass.

"She would be mean to a puppy. I'm going to call Mitzy to make sure Gilbert is okay. You know you want me to."

Joan yawned. She didn't want Sabrina to call Mitzy. Most likely, if she called Mitzy, Joan would have to give up her comfy spot on the sofa and run across town to pick up the dog. This was her favorite episode, where House and Cuddy hooked up. She didn't feel like leaving the sofa, Hugh Laurie, and the nice, fruity Syrah. But the phone was already ringing.

"Mitzy! It's Sabrina! Are they being mean to the puppy?" Sabrina asked. "Not Alonzo, silly, Aerin. Is she being mean to our wittle Gilbert?" Sabrina frowned at Joan. "911? You need to call 911? Is it the puppy, is it okay?" Sabrina was tearing up. Poor Gilbert. They had to call an ambulance for him.

Mitzy grabbed her Birken bag off the floor as it began to ring. Ring! Not a call?! She had half a mind to throw it out the window but it was Sabrina. That was almost as good as 911.

"Sabrina!" she shouted.

"Wait, Sabrina, wait, I'm at the Victorian. Call 911. Alonzo is hurt." Sabrina was saying something else entirely. Mitzy hung up. She didn't have time to waste explaining this to Sabrina. She turned it on again.

Sabrina was still there, she was sniffling. Mitzy hung it up again and waited a few seconds.

She stared at the staircase as she waited. Both sets of arrow posts pointed up, away from the door, and slightly to the left. She tilted her head and followed the line they made carefully.

Both sets of arrows pointed to the narrow wall between the stairs and the parlor.

She dropped the phone and ran to the wall.

She ran her hands up and down the papered surface.

There it was. A panel or a door. She looked up the wall, the height of the two stories she could see. The wall was a dumbwaiter.

The missing jewels were hidden in a closed up dumbwaiter. And they weren't in the basement. Or were they? Maybe the key she found was for operating the dumbwaiter from the basement.

She scratched at the paper with her fingernails, trying to cut into the edge where she could feel the panel but it wasn't working.

She ran to her phone, grabbed it up and hit 911. Emergency services answered right away.

"There's a robbery happening at Smith Boulevard and Baltimore Street, I'm in the house, I'm in danger!" she shouted. The operator spoke calmly and told her police were on their way.

She heard a loud crash in the basement. "Hurry! I think someone's been hurt!" Clinging to the phone, the dog wetting some more and whining constantly, Mitzy ran back to the basement.

She had the Maglite still and swept the room with the light. The basement wide, and long; it took her a few moments to find the men.

Alonzo seemed to have the better of the situation. He was standing, at least. She didn't see Maxim immediately. There was a pile of crates next to Alonzo and Maxim seemed to be under them.

"He's not—dead?" She choked on the word.

"No. He's immobilized, but not dead. I've been trying to work out how he sold himself a house. And then why he was stupid enough to get foreclosed. But he's been pretty pinched about it. I would think at closing the title agent would have noticed that Maxim and Laurence looked a lot alike. There is the chance that Maxim is not in it alone and has a Laurence Mills stand-in for certain jobs." The pile of crates shifted. "I wonder exactly which one of them Sabrina will ID down at the station." Alonzo stood with his arms behind his back and one foot up on a crate. The leg was in some sort of makeshift bandage.

"Alonzo, are you hurt?" Her eyes went wide with concern. She held the flashlight on his leg for a long time. It looked like it was bleeding.

"No, not too bad, sweetie." He pressed his foot down hard on the crate as it rose up again.

"Let me see it." She moved closer.

"It's really not a good time. I'm sort of engaged. Did you have a peek and see if the jewels were still in place?" He was bluffing, but it felt good to have his man down and in suspense.

"You know…" she said, smiling at Alonzo, "I wanted to, but I had to grab a box knife first."

Foreclosed

He couldn't see her features as she spoke, since she held the only light. But he was very excited by what she said. A box knife would be exactly what he would use to access the door to the dumbwaiter. Not that he suspected the infamous and long sought after jewels were hidden behind one layer of wallpaper. But something was hidden there.

"Yes, that would be handy. Though I don't think now is the time." He chatted in a calm voice though he was raging with adrenaline. He could hear sirens as the cops pulled into the driveway.

Mitzy turned and ran back upstairs.

She ran straight out the front door waving her hands madly.

She was breathless, but managed to say, "In the basement. Alonzo has him in the basement. I don't think he's armed." She turned and ran inside. The four police officers followed her lead.

Two of the cops had big flashlights lighting the room. The two in front had stun guns.

"Come out with your hands up!"

Alonzo stepped forward, his hands in the air.

Mitzy wanted to tell them that he was a good guy, but they had left her at the top of the staircase.

The crates clattered to the ground and Maxim Mikhaylichenko slowly stood up. He walked forward and let himself be cuffed.

Mitzy and Alonzo cleared up who they were and why they were there, but ended up being escorted to the station as well.

It wasn't that simple to explain the presence of two Realtors in a foreclosed house at night, especially as they had had a scuffle with the

Mafia. The cops took Maxim's name and the system immediately knew who he was, and most of his aliases.

Foreclosed

Chapter Fourteen

At the station, Gilbert was put into a small plastic animal crate. Mitzy kept the sling around her body to cover the wet and stinking shirt.

Maxim was a person of interest to the cops so she and Alonzo had a detective and a bad cup of coffee each.

"I was interested in the house because the property next door is my rental. If I could sell it to a good neighbor it would protect my other investment." Mitzy sipped her hot, bitter coffee from the plastic lid of the paper cup.

"I see." The detective scratched a note on his paper. "And what brought you into the house this evening?"

She hesitated and he noted it down. "I hadn't been inside yet. So I guess curiosity. I've been talking about the property some on my radio segment—about renovator/foreclosure theft, which I suspected was going on at this property." She paused for another sip of coffee. She sat up straight but she was shaking. They had their man, but she might be in trouble for it still.

"I've heard you a few times on the radio."

When Mitzy didn't volunteer anything new he continued. "Was that all you were interested in this evening?"

"Well...I know I have to be honest, but I feel like a fool saying this out loud. I had done a little reading about this particular house and it seemed to have a mystery associated with it. I sort of wanted to see if there was anything to it." She held her head a little higher, if possible.

"What mystery?" He might have been asking the color of her shoes for all the interest he had in his tone of voice.

"The family that lived in the home for many, many years is associated with a particular set of missing Russian jewelry. And I wondered if there was anything about the house that would..." Mitzy cleared her throat. "I wanted to know if the jewels were in the house." Her face burned with shame as she spoke.

"What did you intend to do if you found the missing jewels?" The cop was writing faster now.

"I didn't have it all planned out, though I did have it in mind to contact a family called Wilber who has some connection to the lost jewels. I thought if there was something at the house, the family would be interested in purchasing the property."

"You didn't want them for yourself?" He made direct eye contact, pen poised over his pad.

"No."

"Why not?"

"What could I do with famous missing jewels? Get into serious trouble, probably. But if the heir of the missing jewels owned the house the jewels were hidden in, they'd be pleased and the value of my rental property would be preserved." She sighed, drank some coffee and wished that she had a more logical reason for being in the house.

"Why was Mr. Miramontes in the house this evening?"

"I don't know."

"Was he looking for the same thing you were after?"

"I don't know. I had gone into the cellar to see what the key I had found fit—"

He interrupted her. "Describe the key."

She did and he scratched more notes.

"What happened when you went into the cellar?" the detective asked.

"I had a small flashlight and looked around. I saw a man I didn't know. He addressed me and then attacked me. Alonzo Miramontes came down the stairs shortly after and was also attacked." She told him as many details of the attack as she could recall, right down to the dog piddling on her shirt.

"And you didn't know that Maxim Mikhaylichenko or Alonzo Miramontes would be in the house this evening?"

"No, sir."

"Thank you, Mitzy. That will be all. We'll contact you at a later date."

"I can go now?" Her head spun. She had expected him to put her in a cell, not send her home.

"Yup. We have your statement and that you want to press charges against him for the attack. We will get a hold of you. If you think of anything new that we need to know, please call in." He stood and motioned to the door. Mitzy exited and sat in the waiting room, waiting for the puppy and for Alonzo.

Alonzo came out of another room, similar to the one Mitzy had been in. He carried out the dog carrier and offered Mitzy his arm.

They left the police station in silence.

Alonzo handed Mitzy into the taxi and then sat beside her. "Did they make the house a crime scene?" she asked him after a while.

"I don't think so. Unless Maxim says he was there to steal the missing jewels." Alonzo stretched his arm across the back of the bench seat.

"I had to tell them I was there for the jewels." She tipped her head back onto his arm. "What did you tell them?"

"I told them that I thought you had gone to the house and I was worried for your safety. I told them that a number of things had happened, such as the attack on Sabrina. I told them I drove by the property, saw your car, and went in to make sure you were okay."

"You did? You told them that?" She was still wrapping her mind around the idea of Alonzo being on her side.

"I had to tell them the truth."

"Are you still going to buy the house for Carmella?"

"Are you going to sell it to the Wilbers?"

"I don't know. It seems like the missing jewels should be theirs. But then, if they are found they might need to be returned to the Russian Government." She watched the line of apple trees, with white blossoms shining under the street lights as they drove down the road. "How did you know that Laurence Mills was Maxim Mikhaylichenko?"

"I've worked with Laurence on a few jobs. He knew everybody and everybody knew him. But he wasn't a 'Mills.' For starters, he had that heavy accent. Plus he knew a lot of people in the building trades that had bad reputations."

"And you just put two and two together?"

"Nope. I called one of my more disreputable friends. He looked into it."

"It wasn't Bruce was it?"

"Bruce was very helpful. But Bruce is solid gold. Disreputable is the last word for him. I don't think you need to know who I called. Probably not safe."

"I've had enough of not safe for right now."

"You buy the house, Mitzy. Buy it for cash. Then decide what to do, if you happen to find something of value in the house."

"Would that be safe? And could I really afford it right now?" She guessed at the price the bank would ask and knew it was a bigger chunk than she wanted to take out of her cash reserve.

"I think Maxim was working alone on the jewels job."

"So the house is safe?"

"Probably."

They sat quietly for a bit longer.

At Mitzy's parents' house, he opened the door for her. "We can afford it together. We could own it tomorrow."

Mitzy took his arm and walked up to her parents' door. She had the puppy carrier in one hand and her purse over her shoulder. She needed a shower and a cry on her mom's shoulder. "Give it the overnight test, Alonzo. Don't decide right now."

He wrapped his arms around her thin shoulders and held her, urine soaked shirt and all, for a few moments. As soon as she was safe in the house he took the taxi back home.

Wednesday morning, with deeply depleted cash reserves and afraid they had just made a huge mistake, Mitzy and Alonzo met on the front porch of their new house.

He opened the door with the key and let Mitzy in first. She didn't have her purple Birken bag today or her smart purple business suit. They both wore boots and blue jeans and clothes you could hunt for treasure in.

She had her cell phone in her pocket, though Maxim was locked up at least until his trial. She also had her personal tool chest, in purple. Alonzo had his as well.

They both went straight to the parlor side dumbwaiter and began pulling off wallpaper. It was tedious and took a straight edge, mineral spirits and a scraper. But the door appeared eventually.

Mitzy took the box knife and sliced into the layers of paint that had glued the door shut.

She was shaking as she loosened three sides of the panel.

"You're going to slice yourself, give me that." Alonzo took the knife from her. He worked with a steady hand.

They pulled together on the door until it popped open.

The small box for delivering things up and down the height of the house was made of perfect walnut. It was stained a deep brown and had clear wood grain. It had been sealed up and unused for so many years that it looked new.

But it was empty.

Alonzo pressed on all sides of the box, looking for a secret panel.

"Move over. I want to see." Mitzy nudged with her hip.

Alonzo pressed on the top of the dumbwaiter and it lifted on a hinge.

Then he turned to Mitzy and kissed her full on the mouth.

Her head spun. Her heart beat like thunder.

She wrapped her arms around him, letting her fingers thread through his thick, black hair.

Then she pulled away.

He wrapped his arm around her waist. "It doesn't matter what's in here, Mitzy."

"No. It doesn't." The warmth of his hand on her waist was worth whatever she would find behind the secret door.

It was everything.

He reached in again, held the trap door up.

She slipped her hand inside.

She felt something soft, like velvet. It was hard to grasp with one hand, but she managed to pull the object down into the dumbwaiter.

A heavy purple velvet bag landed with a thud and a poof of dust.

She stepped back. "There it is."

He urged her forward with a little push.

She picked up the bag carefully, weighing it in her hands and then spilled the contents onto the floor of the dumbwaiter.

The remains of a once great jewelry collection lay before her. Two rings, two small pendants on thick gold chains, and a broach of deep blue sapphires. Mitzy exhaled, speechless.

Alonzo eyed Mitzy, her lean body in casual clothes, hair pulled back into a soft, loose pony tail. Her eyes were brilliant blue and her cheeks were flushed with excitement. He wrapped his arms around her in a bear hug, lifting her a little off of her feet.

She every inch of her body shivered.

A tap sounded at the front door.

Alonzo dropped his arms and Mitzy slipped down to her feet again.

The door opened.

"You made it." Mitzy stepped forward and extended her hand.

A man in a sharp black suit shook her hand and nodded.

"Ambassador?" Alonzo asked.

"Yes, yes. I'm here from the embassy. Call me Eduard."

"Eduard Ivanovich?" Mitzy held out her hand for his ID.

"Of course." He held out an ID badge and looked around the room. "Have you had any success yet?"

"We have." Mitzy passed him the jewelry, nestled on top of the velvet bag.

"You've done the right thing," Eduard said. "You wouldn't believe the trouble we've had repatriating the national treasure."

Alonzo snorted. "We just might."

"Well, yes. I suppose you would." He cleared his throat and looked over the collection. Then he set his titanium briefcase on the floor and knelt down beside it.

He laid the pieces in the case one at a time. Then he pulled a sheet of paper from his pocket and unfolded it. He compared the jewelry with the list. He cleared his throat again. "This looks like what we were hoping for." He snapped the case shut and locked it.

He stood up and brushed the knees of his slacks with his hand. After he straightened out he pulled a card out of his pocket and passed it to Alonzo. "If anything else comes up you need to let me know."

Mitzy reached across for the card. "Of course. If anything else shows up. We will get a receipt for all of this, right?"

Eduard heaved a dramatic sigh. "Yes, of course." He mumbled something about American paperwork as he opened his case again. He took out a carbon form and filled it in.

Foreclosed

Mitzy tapped her toe while he wrote.

Eduard pulled the form apart and handed the top sheet to Alonzo.

Alonzo smiled and passed it to Mitzy.

Eduard folded the remaining sheets and tucked them back in the case. He gave one last look around the front of the house, shook his head, and left.

"Maxim Mikhaylichenko is in prison now," Mitzy said. "And the jewels are on their way back to Russia. That's the end of it."

"The museum had to give back the money, didn't they?" Alonzo asked.

"They didn't collect any, actually. But it's no matter. They could sell half a painting and make more than they did from the jewelry."

"They got a lot of press though," Alonzo said.

"And any press is good press. They'll recover." Mitzy looked up to the top of the staircase. Handing the jewelry over like that had dampened her spirit.

"And you will recover?" Alonzo asked, his voice hushed and concerned.

Mitzy took a deep breath. "I'm fine. I got knocked around a little. But what's that in light of the grand scheme? What I want to know is will the economy recover?"

Alonzo nodded in agreement. He knocked on the wall nearest to him. "It's got good bones," he said.

"It's a beautiful home." She sighed a little, but smiled. "It will make a great little inn."

"You won't be sorry." Alonzo leaned his elbow on the wall and looked Mitzy over again with a smile.

"You're right. I won't be. We've started this now. We have to be a success."

Foreclosed

Traci Tyne Hilton

Eminent Domain

A Mitzy Neuhaus Mystery

1

The floorboard crumbled under Mitzy's first step. She extracted her boot, ignoring the scratches on the new leather and said, "Replace floor."

Alonzo Miramontes offered Mitzy his hand and directed her to a firmer spot in the upper attic room they were touring. "Replace floor," he repeated, making a note on his iPhone.

The mansion on Baltimore Street had hooked Mitzy earlier in the year. As a Realtor she knew the broke-down mansion was a great commission waiting to happen. She also saw potential every time she looked at it. It could be a magnificent building with a little work. And since she owned the little rental house next door, potential for the mansion was potential property value for her as well. As icing on the cake, all that renovation work would mean jobs for her friends.

Foreclosed

But Mitzy was realizing the word 'renovation' was insufficient. An argument could be made for just tearing the old house down. The untamed acres of property and ramshackle house that had consumed her mind were now consuming all of her capital as she, her new boyfriend Alonzo, and his sister Carmella converted it into an inn.

Buying the house had been the action of a heated moment. Alonzo and Mitzy had tried to buy it out from under each other, but found that the Mafia didn't want either of them to have it. There was a little secret in the house, earlier that spring—a stash of missing jewels, from the Russian royal family, the Romanovs.

Mitzy was the best Realtor in Portland. A millionaire by 30. She didn't get to the top by making mistakes. But in the thrill of the battle for the jewels, the house, and their lives, she and Alonzo had skimped on a few home buying technicalities. In fact, she had broken her favorite rule as a Realtor: Due Diligence. Mitzy took her job as a Realtor seriously. She wore her purple blazer with the company logo with pride. She wore her matching purple fingernails with pride too.

But being a Realtor was more than just owning a business to Mitzy. It was her life's blood. The due diligence she had forgotten was the inspection. A mortgage requires an inspection, but cash can move mountains. Who needs an inspection when you are hunting for missing jewels? This was the first time Mitzy had discovered a whole floor of living space in a building after purchasing it.

Turning the property into an inn was Carmella and Alonzo's dream. Since falling in love with Alonzo she had fallen in with this dream. But really, the love part only complicated the business start up. Mitzy fully intended to get beyond the drama of the mansion and the jewels and the Mafia and get back to selling homes as soon as the inn was up and running.

The business partners were dealing with the servants' quarters on the top floor of the house today. The floor that had been a complete surprise. Mitzy was becoming convinced as she sketched plans yet again for the rooms upstairs, that some mountains should just stay put.

The Victorian mansion had five bed rooms right below the storage attic. It was enough space to house a butler, cook, and a few maids. Also on that floor was a larger room that must have been a school room or nursery.

"We need one large suite with extensive private accommodations, bath, sauna, living room, and big screen TV," Carmella, Alonzo's sister and future inn manager said.

"No," Alonzo said.

"It's the top floor. It needs to be posh," Carmella said.

"Can we even get a spa up here?" Mitzy asked eyeing the narrow stairs and low ceilings.

"Lift it in through the window. It doesn't matter how we do it; it just needs to be done." Carmella drew a line across the window with her pointer finger.

"We are not plumbing a spa up here. It's too expensive. We'd have to reinforce all the floor joists. Can't do it. We'd have to get new permits. These rooms should be offices and storage," Alonzo said.

"No," Carmella said, shaking her head. "I am the inn manager and the design consultant. We can't waste all of this space on storage and offices. The more rooms open, the more money we make."

Mitzy was measuring windows with her keychain measuring tape and responded without thinking. "The more we advertise the more money we make."

"Focus, Mitzy," Alonzo said. "And you," he said to his sister, "are not our design consultant. You had better not expect to be paid for design consulting. You are not a designer."

"You invited me here for my opinion. I assume it is my opinion on design and not on what to have for lunch." She tossed her thick black pony tail and turned her head to the window. "This is the best room in the house because it is the top room. The offices need to be downstairs so I am available to our guests," Carmella said.

"We're turning the staff staircase into an elevator," Mitzy said.

"Focus," Alonzo snapped.

"I am focused. Don't be such a jerk. We are putting an elevator here, so guest access to the top floor wouldn't be a problem." She walked through the doorway into the hall, looking up and down its length. "But fitting out a suite would be." She raised her voice to be heard. "If this is opened to guests at all it needs two washrooms. But if we don't have sleeping space it wouldn't have to be full on-suite baths. For two toilets and two sinks we wouldn't have to reinforce floor joists, etc. The nursery is large and we could open up into the other small rooms." Mitzy walked back into the room with her partners.

Alonzo shook his head, eyes lowered to a paper he was holding. "We have all of our estimates," he said.

"We left the servants' quarters 'to be decided,'" Mitzy said. "We might as well decide now."

"Because we don't have enough to do?" Alonzo said.

"I have two ideas," Mitzy began. "The first is the best. We could turn this into a banquet room. We would just need two bathrooms. The ceilings are low so it wouldn't be very grand, but we could make it stylish and offer it as part of our wedding packages." She paused and looked at Alonzo to see how he liked it. "Or we could turn it into a business conference room and fit it out like a smoking room or library, or that kind of manly thing."

"We do need to add those bathrooms, no matter what we do," Alonzo said, thumping the floor boards with his booted foot. "Do you know what it costs to reinforce these old beams?"

"We could get a lot more money for it as a honeymoon suite," Carmella said.

Mitzy observed Carmella. Her peevish expression was so exactly like her brother's. Her lips were pursed and her thick eyebrows drawn over her big black eyes. Her shoulders were thrown back and she stood with her feet planted shoulder width apart.

"We'll keep that idea in mind, Carmella. But as far as we can tell off hand, it isn't in the budget." Mitzy patted her fluffy blond curls as she thought. Top floor was top floor. But these spaces had been servant's quarters. Small rooms, small windows, low ceilings. Even converting them to a conference room would require larger windows and disturb the historic integrity of the façade.

"Carmella," Mitzy asked, "what would you charge per night for your top floor honeymoon suite?"

"At minimum, $400 a night," Carmella said.

"And what would you charge for your smallest room?" Mitzy asked.

"Nothing in this hotel will be less than $175 a night."

Mitzy pointed as she counted the rooms. "Then one, two, three, four, five, junior-rooms with shared baths off the hall and continental breakfast in the nursery at $100 dollars a night, would be more profitable than one large suite at four hundred." Mitzy smiled. This new plan was her favorite by far. "If you had the large suite rented every weekend in June and half of July and August the inn would make $3200 a year on this space. If we averaged renting half these rooms half of the weekends for the year this space would bring in $5250 a year. What do you think?"

"Can we get away with five bedrooms and shared bathrooms?" Alonzo asked.

"Sure. The McMennimins hotels do it," Mitzy said.

"McMennimins hotels are destinations. We won't have a movie theater, a micro-brewery, or golfing," Carmella said.

"True," Alonzo said. "But I think we could get the permits. I'd rather have a handful of rooms to rent than a conference room that was always empty."

"Me too, I think we could do it. It would be so much cheaper. All we have to do is put in the bathrooms, new flooring, and paint. I'll draw up the plans and estimates," Mitzy said.

"So we're just going to do your plan then?" Carmella said.

"Yes," Alonzo replied turning to go down the stairs.

"I'm sorry," Mitzy said.

Carmella's shoulders drooped for just a moment. She pulled them back up though and glared at her brother's retreating figure.

"We just can't afford your idea, even though it is awesome." Mitzy paused and looked at Carmella. Carmella turned away, crossing her arms on her chest. With a shrug, Mitzy started her trek down the flights of stairs to the main floor.

Alonzo was arguing in the foyer with two well dressed men. Through the front windows Mitzy saw two black Lincolns with tinted windows. And a police car.

"What's going on here?" Mitzy rushed down the last few steps and interjected herself into the argument.

"I've got it, Mitzy," Alonzo said. He stood with his feet apart and his arms crossed over his broad chest. "Until you show us a court order you're not taking anything from this property."

A tall, thin, man with wire rim glasses and sparse blond hair peered around the foyer before he spoke. "I don't think you realize the seriousness of the situation. I don't think you realize who you are working with here."

Foreclosed

"I realize," Alonzo said, dropping his voice an octave and speaking slowly like to a child, "that you are attempting to seize our property without the legal authority. I realize that I am going to escort you off of our property now."

Mitzy had moved to the front door, keeping the heels of her boots quiet on the wood floor, while the strangers had their stand off with Alonzo. She opened the door and a gust of fall scented wind blew into the room. "After you," she said with a false smile, gritting her teeth.

No one moved.

The thin man stepped towards Alonzo. "I can see you've never worked with the FBI before."

A local policeman stepped in through the front door. He stalked into the room, leading with his forehead and stood between the shorter, dark haired FBI man and the thin, reedy one. He glared around the room, turning to take everyone in. When he saw Mitzy his face burst into a grin and he puffed out his chest. "You're Mitzy Neuhaus!" he said, his voice rising like a choir boy. "I saw you on TV this morning."

Mitzy turned on her hundred watt smile and joined the officer in the middle of the room. "Hey there," she said fluttering her eyelashes and pursing her pink lips. Alonzo frowned.

The thin blond agent frowned as well.

"Is this THE Victorian?" the cop asked. "The one you found the missing jewels in?"

"It sure is," Mitzy said.

Traci Tyne Hilton

"Such a bummer that you had to turn them all over to the authorities. You bought 'em, you should get to keep 'em." The cop shook his head and looked around the house again, eyes wide with admiration.

"You have to come back and visit us once we've opened the inn," Mitzy said. "It's going to be gorgeous."

"Will do," the cop said with a nod. "You done in here?" the cop asked the FBI agents in his deep, policeman voice.

"No, we are not done here," the thin one said biting off the ends of his words.

"These guys have work to do," the cop said. "I suggest you finish up and move on. I have work to do too."

The thin man sucked in a breath that flared out his nostrils. "I am here for the items on this list. As you learned when you turned in the Romanov jewelry collection, you do not have a choice. As you can see I've brought the local law to enforce the order, though if you knew anything at all, I didn't have to bring them." He glared at the officer who was still chatting up Mitzy.

"Come back with a warrant and take whatever the judge says you can take." Alonzo walked forward, forcing the two men in suits to retreat to the open door. The cop followed them out.

"You don't realize what it means to frustrate the FBI, do you?" the thin agent said.

"I am so sorry you are feeling frustrated," Mitzy said. "But that has nothing to do with us. We have a building to renovate."

Foreclosed

The agents hesitated in the gravel drive. Their cars stood waiting for them. The beefy one spoke for the first time. "We'll be back," he said and then opened the door of his black Lincoln.

The tall thin agent's shoulders slumped at his partner's ridiculous comment. Collins hated working with new agents. The agents slammed the doors to their cars shut, and kicked up the gravel with their wheels as they drove off of the property.

Mitzy turned away from the exiting cars and looked at Alonzo with fear in her wide, blue eyes. "Those guys were the FBI? What on earth did they want?"

"They want everything in the house that is not nailed down," Alonzo said.

A small green Prius squealed into the driveway. A middle-aged man with spiky hair and thick black glasses popped out. "Hey, guys," he said with a big toothy grin.

Alonzo looked at the man once, turned and went back into the house.

"I'm Geo from the city council," the man said. "Let's talk about your property." He walked over to Mitzy and offered to shake her hand.

Mitzy put a business card in his hand. "Call my assistant and make an appointment," she said. She turned on her boot heel and followed Alonzo into the house.

Traci Tyne Hilton

Traci Tyne Hilton is the author of *The Mitzy Neuhaus Mystery Series*, *The Plain Jane Mystery Series*, *The Hearts to God Romance Series* and one of the authors in *The Tangle Saga* series of science fiction novellas.

She was the Mystery/Suspense Category winner for the 2012 Christian Writers of the West Phoenix Rattler Contest, a finalist for Speculative Fiction in the same contest, and has a Drammy from the Portland Civic Theatre Guild. Traci serves as the Vice President of the Portland chapter of the American Christian Fiction Writers Association.

Traci earned a degree in History from Portland State University and still lives in the rainiest part of the Pacific Northwest with her husband the mandolin playing funeral director, their two daughters, and their dog, Dr. Watson.

Find more of Traci Tyne Hilton's work at tracihilton.com
or connect with her at tracityne@hotmail.com
and on Facebook!

Foreclosed

Traci Tyne Hilton

Cozy Christian Mysteries

by

The Mitzy Neuhaus Mysteries

Eminent Domain

Mitzy Neuhaus is dying to get back to business as usual, but The Worst Economy Since The Great Depression has just about killed her real estate business. But when the excessive interest of the FBI, city planners, and possibly the Mafia, threaten to derail Mitzy's plans things really get dangerous…

Buyer's Remorse

Mitzy Neuhaus had an easier time selling her condo before the mystery buyer "bought it" on her patio. Mitzy stumbled over the body and knew she had to get involved in the case—if only because the corpse was a dead ringer for herself.

At first it seemed like a clear case of mistaken identity and Mitzy feared the Mafia wasn't done with her yet. But digging into the life of the dead buyer uncovered a peculiar little dress shop where nothing added up.

Can Mitzy untangle the mystery before she ends up with her own case of buyer's remorse?

The Plain Jane Mysteries
Good, Clean Murder

Living on her own for her first time, Bible school student Jane cleans houses to make ends meet. But being independent brings big trials, like falling for a handsome professor, dealing with an obnoxious roommate, and then there's the dead bodies…

Who knew being housekeeper to wealthy owners of a Roly Burger franchise would mean sweeping up clues to their death, while ministering to the needs of their heirs?

This is one big mess that Jane is intent on cleaning up before things get even worse.

Dirty Little Murder

College student and housekeeper Jane Adler dreams of being a missionary but the road to the 10/40 window is littered with corpses.

Jane found the most recent body floating in the hot tub at her newest client's house. The dead guy was a notorious flirt and carouser. Had his romantic shenanigans gotten him killed?

Cleaning up a murder was bad enough, but Jane's love life was a mess too. Usually absence makes the heart grow fonder, but her boyfriend Isaac's overseas teaching job seems to be driving them apart.

On top of it all she's been hand selected by her church as a candidate for one of their few fully funded missionary support positions. But can she solve a murder, keep her boyfriend, and follow her dream all at the same time?

Bright New Murder

Homeless preschoolers, angry protesters, frozen yogurt, and murder.

Jane Adler is keen to try on her detective hat, and the dead lady at the Christmas fundraiser is her perfect shot.

Timing is everything and this murder was timed perfectly to destroy her best friend Jake's growing Fro-Yo business. He's a great friend–just a friend, honest– and she owes him a favor or two.

But discovering who would want to kill the town's favorite preschool teacher is messy business, and Jane doesn't have a moment to waste!

CPSIA information can be obtained at www.ICGtesting.com
Printed in the USA
LVOW07s1931240215

428161LV00010B/863/P